M000164123

BEING BETJEMAN(N)

By the same author

fiction
Wilfred and Eileen
The English Lover
In Flight
Come Back
Summer in February
Night Windows
The Churchill Secret

non-fiction
Good Enough? (with Chris Cowdrey)
The Learning Game
The Following Game

BEING BETJEMAN(N)

Jonathan Smith

Galileo Publishers, Cambridge

Published by Galileo Publishers
16 Woodlands Road
Great Shelford
Cambridge CB22 5LW UK
www.galileopublishing.co.uk

Distributed in the USA by SCB Distributors
&
in Australia by Peribo Pty Ltd

ISBN 978-1-912916-290

The author and publishers are grateful to John Murray for
permission to quote extensively from Betjeman's verse

First edition
© 2020 Galileo Publishers

The moral right of the author has been asserted
© 2020 Jonathan Smith

All rights reserved. This book is sold subject to the
condition that it shall not, by way of trade or otherwise, be lent,
resold, hired out or otherwise circulated in any form of binding or
cover other than that in which it is published and without a
similar condition including this condition being imposed
on the subsequent purchaser.

Printed in the EU

For Bruce Young

*The quickest way to start a punch-up between two
British literary critics is to ask them what they think
of the poems of Sir John Betjeman.*
Philip Larkin

Being Betjeman kept me going.
Benjamin Whitrow

PART ONE

1 | SWALLOWING THE SPIDER

When I was young and at university, a clever scholar I knew always wrote the letter r, the lower case r, as a capital. WheReveR the letteR appeaRed in a woRd he did it. FoR a yeaR oR moRe I then found that I was doing the same. My mother sometimes said to other people, and in my hearing, that I had always been a rather impressionable little boy, and while she was on the topic of my character, and taking her time about it, she would go on to say that I was prone to putting some people on a pedestal.

Many years later, when I was a teacher, a clever colleague of mine had a slight stammer, an impediment which was barely more than a hesitancy that lasted a few seconds, before he spoke with a strong and emphatic flow. I waited hungrily for his words, as one had to, and they were usually worth the waiting. For a while I then found that I was allowing a similar pause before I spoke, a full pause but not too long, and I noticed that people were now more focused and more attentive if not more impressed by the weight of what I had to say.

As an impressionable writer I have, it occurs to me, been all sorts of people. I have followed each and every one of them closely, spying on them, eavesdropping on their conversations, catching their rhythms of speech, imitating them, checking up on them to see if they told the truth, wearing their clothes and, in a nutshell, pretending to be them.

They are a motley, larger than life, bunch. I am not sure what this list says about me, and I certainly did not put them on pedestals, but in my time I have been Albert Speer, Hitler's architect and armaments minister, W.E. Henley, the one-legged poet on whom Robert Louis Stevenson based his Long John

Silver, Winston Churchill, August Rodin, Alfred Munnings, the controversial painter, and (not too taxing, this last one) a moderately famous headmaster.

For months, for years while doing this, I often felt I was a nobody and they were all somebodies, and I found I preferred being a somebody, enjoyed being them more than simply (whatever this meant) being me.

I'm nobody! Who are you?
Are you nobody, too?

Then there's a pair of us – don't tell!
They'd banish us you know.

As with any other writer of novels and plays I have, of course, also 'made up' many characters from scratch (whatever 'made up' means). For as long as it took I walked in their shoes too, and changed my age and cross-dressed, and I have identified with – fallen in love with – any number of female characters, wonderful women, and you have no idea what we've done to each other behind closed doors.

For parts of my later life, and particularly in recent years – and this brings me to the matter in hand – I have been reading and searching for and obsessed by the poet John Betjeman. For spells no other writer has got a look in. He was, he is, so accessible and so knowable and so charming and so vulnerable and yet – and yet – he eludes me, and he bothers me, especially as a father and as a son.

As well as bothering me, this developing obsession has, to put it mildly, vexed some of my bookish friends. Only the other day one wrote to me, asking me upfront and with some exasperation, what is this thing I have about John Betjeman. And he has by no means been alone in asking. What on earth, he wants to know, led me to land on the poet in the first place, and how come I have stayed a loyal fan all these years? I'm not sure I can answer all this to his satisfaction but it may be easier if I quote his latest letter in full. The tone, by the way, with its hint of animus, is not untypical:

Dear Jonathan,

You and Betjeman: forgive me, but I am as intrigued by the affinity as worried by the possession. What drew you in? At the risk of being over-simplistic and overly biographical I cannot for the life of me spot any parallels. There was no rift that I am aware of between you and your father. There is no rift that I can see between you and your son. You have a limited interest in architecture or trains or churches or fallen priests. You aren't drawn to girls who look like boys. You don't believe in God, except when you're frightened, but then that goes for most people.

Perhaps you have always been a lover of light verse? Not that I have noticed. You have never been one to sit with girls in golf club car parks; indeed, you avoid golf clubs full stop. Although it sometimes seems obligatory for writers, you were not bullied at school, or if you were you have kept very quiet about it. You are not a social climber. You have shown no wish to be part of the country house set and you do not hobnob with royalty. You do not have two wives. You cannot write poetry, but you can catch a cricket ball.

I don't get it.

Robert

Anyway, be that as it may, one morning I sat down in my hut and started to write a piece in Betjeman's voice – as I understood it and heard it – and I felt I was, in quite a disturbing way, inhabiting his skin. In front of the mirror and on solitary walks I spoke out loud as him, and I'm not too bad a mimic.

But it was a much deeper thing than merely taking him off or ventriloquising. In the middle of the night, wide awake myself, wide awake as him, I would wonder whose bed he was in, his wife's or his lover's, and was it always with a woman, or only with women who looked like boys?

I'm not sure if it was partly the long years of my pursuit or my gradually intensifying appropriation which tipped me over the edge, or if it would have happened anyway, if the wheels were overdue to come off, but in the summer of 2016, for the first time in my life, while being Betjeman, I broke down, although no doctor now uses that term. Anyway, whichever way you care to describe it, I could not cope.

★

How can I capture what happened to me without the clichés? How can I admit it without being embarrassing? Well, to start with a cliché: it just came over me. And the thing is, I did not see it coming. For a long time I was all right in a normal everyday-ish sort of way, and the next minute I wasn't. It was as if I was walking along the beach, a Betjeman beach with bladderwrack, say Daymer Bay in North Cornwall, with the breeze on my face and a ginger beer foam at my feet, enjoying one of life's simple pleasures, with the sea on my left, and the tide going slowly out, with the soft slippy sand of the dunes on my right, and I remember a bulky black Labrador had just bounded past me chasing a yellow tennis ball, I can see its ribcage now and its yellow teeth and somebody in the distance was calling 'Good boy, Barney, good boy', and all was more or less OK with me and the world, when I felt my feet slowing down and my eyes staring. I could not stop staring.

Hang on, what was going on? I had a horrible taste in my mouth. I must have swallowed something disgusting. But it was worse than that because, as with Leontes in *The Winter's*

12

Tale, I had not only swallowed something disgusting, a live spider in my glass of red wine, but I had seen it slipping down my throat. I was staring, staring as if I were being very rude to someone, or as if I were transfixed. I was caught in a storm which came from nowhere. The tide had turned and I was in it up to my neck.

Then I found I was in tears. I could not stop them. I did not ask for it, any of it, I had no say in it. I felt I had been poisoned.

★

I have just re-read that last bit and it's not quite right either, but it's the best I can do: Betjeman and my mental health, in ways that I am still trying to understand, seemed somehow to fuse together. Quite suddenly, or it felt quite suddenly, although I now realise it was not sudden, I did not know who I was or, as Dusty Springfield sang, with her big eyes and her lashings of mascara, I did not know what to do with myself. *I just don't know what to do with myself.* I felt lost, even when I was with my family and close friends. I was without ballast and with no anchor, apart from poetry.

And then, to top it all off, just as I was beginning to feel more in control of my life, just as I was beginning to handle my anxiety disorder, I developed Parkinson's, which, as it so happens, was to be Betjeman's final disease.

2 | MONTAIGNE, 1580

Few are more aware of the power of the imagination than I am. Everyone feels its force, but some are turned upside down by it. It makes such an intense impression on me that I prefer to avoid it altogether than try to resist it… the very sight of someone else's pain causes me real pain, and my body often takes on the sensations of the person I am with. Another person's cough tickles my lungs and throat. I'm more reluctant to visit those I love and am bound to care for, when they're sick, than those I care less about, and mean less to me. I adopt their disease that troubles me, and make it my own.

Translated by Iain McGilchrist

3 | CAMBRIDGE, MICHAELMAS, 1960

I have been 'on' Betjeman for most of my life, mostly under cover. In October 1960 I went up to Cambridge as a freshman, that's nearly sixty years ago now, blimey, and that autumn, browsing in Bowes and Bowes bookshop (no longer Bowes and Bowes), I bought a first edition of *Summoned By Bells*, John Betjeman's verse autobiography, or his *epic* as he (ironically, I suspect) called it.

In it he describes his suburban childhood, his only-childhood in North London. He tells us of his early life in 31 West Hill, N6. He takes us into his Highgate world, with his deaf upright father, his garrulous hypochondriac mother, the family's factory in Pentonville, his boarding school and undergraduate days, his happy times in Trebetherick, Cornwall, ah, Cornwall, you can't beat it, can you, and his brief and unlikely spell (where we leave him) as a schoolteacher and master i/c cricket, a game he had never played and of which he was terrified.

He bares his soul, or so it seems to me, and though I am a bit wary of those who too easily bare their souls, I was swept along, and he ends his 'epic' while still a very young man, believing that most of the important things in life tend to have happened to you by the time you get to twenty-eight. And he might be right. It's a small part of life we really live. Hang on. *It's a small part of life we lead*. Is that a line of Seneca's? Or quoted by Seneca? I don't know, or if I ever did.

Anyway, I stood there, in late 1960, at the Bowes and Bowes bookshop counter, holding Betjeman's distilled and edited life, for what else is an autobiography, holding the book I was about to buy. It felt just right in my hands, and that is so important, the feel of a book, the smell of a book, especially a hardback book, now all yours, as you open it for the first time. It was beautiful. (I say it *was* beautiful rather than it *is* beautiful because the book I bought in 1960 was lent or lost or, who knows, probably nicked from me many years ago.) The dust jacket was, as I remember, an elegant design, a simple creamy beige cover, with just the title, then three bells and the poet's name underneath. Understated, perfect.

Back in my college rooms I put it proudly on my shelf for all the world to see, centrally placed in the very small collection of books I then owned.

Everyone who came into my room and saw it, laughed.

-Betjeman?

-Yes.

-John Bet-je-man?

-Yes.

-You're not serious? *Phone for the fish-knives, Norman.*

-What do you mean?

-You've just been out and *bought* a Betjeman?

-Yes, well, I've –

-You're not saying he's any good?

-I've always –

-You *are*?

-I think he –

-For God's sake, you Welsh git, he's a bloody joke.

-Is he? You think so?

-*Come, friendly bombs, and fall on Slough.*

-What's wrong with that?

–I mean, Jonathan, come *on*.

After a week or so of this scoffing I took *Summoned By Bells* off my bookshelf and stuffed it in a bedroom drawer, under my socks and underpants, under the radar, where even I couldn't see it. It was that embarrassing.

4 | TENNESSEE WILLIAMS

Three years later, in the early summer of 1963, I was working in a lemonade factory in a very different Cambridge. From eight o'clock in the morning until five in the evening I sat on a plastic seat next to a conveyor belt. I had never been in a place like it before or since, and I had never known such a noise.

On my right-hand side were crates full of empty pop bottles piled high, and I had to lift the sticky empties out of the crates and place them, two at a time, four across, neck down on to the moving belt, where they shook and rattled and clinked noisily on their way to be rinsed and then refilled with Lemonade or Orangeade or Raspberryade or Raspberry Plus. There was no difference, an old factory hand confided in me, between Raspberryade and Raspberry Plus. They just changed the labels, he said, and charged more for the Raspberry Plus.

I had finished the academic year in debt, unable to pay either my Bowes and Bowes bill (books) or my Buttery bill (drink). My father, a primary school head teacher in Bristol, made it clear that he was not going to settle either, which was irritating and fair enough. So I spent my early summer days of 1963 on a plastic seat next to the conveyor belt in a lemonade factory and, as I'd had to vacate my college rooms, spent my nights sleeping on the floor of Terry's room above the Indian restaurant in Petty Cury. This was in the days when Petty Cury was a narrow medieval street, and much closer to the one mentioned in Pepys' Diary than the pedestrianised shopping mall it now is.

Terry was a bricklayer. I'd got to know him in the 'town' pubs around the Market Square, pubs in which undergraduates were advisedly thin on the ground. Terry wore a black leather jacket and black leather trousers and kept his motorbike in the tiny cobbled yard below his room. If you are of a certain age, think of a young Marlon Brando. Think *The Wild One* (1953). Think *On the Waterfront* (1954). Terry, of course, always had a girl. He had swagger. He had the glamorous air of the outlaw; I had the air of the Larkin bloke who ducks down behind the counter of the saloon bar just before the shooting begins. We got on very well, Terry and I, we hit it off, and after a couple of pints we would start to sing lines from Eddie Cochran songs to or rather at each other, usually – no, not usually, inevitably – *Three Steps to Heaven:*

Terry: *Step one – you find a girl to love*

Me: *Step two – she falls in love with you*

Terry: *Step three – you kiss and hold her tightly*

Both of us: *Yeah! That sure feels like heaven to me*

We made each other laugh and we were proud to know each other. He once said to me, as he was dragging me out of a King Street pub after he thought I was getting 'a bit lippy' with a local, that I *needed looking after.*

As far as I could see, Terry did not read anything apart from the occasional glance at a newspaper, whereas I, safe from academic snobbery and undergraduate mockery and lacerating laughter, was now back to reading my Betjeman, back to my guilty secret.

It took me nearly six weeks to earn enough money to pay off my book bill and my drink bill mainly because I was still spending heavily on books and drink (and anything left went on seeing exclusively foreign films at the flicks). Terry was surprised that he had to point out such a simple thing to a student, to 'a grad', surprised that 'a college boy who read books' like me couldn't see the debt issue for himself. I could see it, but I couldn't or wouldn't do anything about it. I had a books and drink problem as, in a less damaging way, I still do. I still can't get through a single day without either and I have never been able to do so since I left school at eighteen. Spells in hospital don't count.

Working in that lemonade factory was the closest I have ever come to being a character in a Tennessee Williams play. It was claustrophobic. It was airless and hot and you could smell the sticky pop and we workers could smell each other. We were cheek by jowl. The whole place was simmering with random violence and sexual edge and all the necessary oppositions were in place for a high octane drama: there was hysteria v indifference, machismo v effeminacy, and neuroses v ruthlessness. They were there on every page of Tennessee Williams, these oppositions, and I came across them in the flesh every day in that Cambridge lemonade factory.

All right, there was no Marlon Brando playing Stanley Kowalski in a tight white T-shirt; there was no one saying 'I'm not a Polack, I'm from Poland, but what I am is one hundred percent American', and there was no Vivien Leigh lighting the candles with her fluttery hand gestures. But I did see a ten foot high stack of crates deliberately pushed over just as a very attractive woman was walking past. She wasn't badly hurt. She had a bruised back and a few cuts to her arms. From my seat high above the shop floor on the conveyor belt I saw who did it and I saw (and can still see) the slow motion sway of the toppling crates, but I said nothing. I wasn't daft. I was D and D, deaf and dumb. I felt I was in a film. I was in a scene from *On the Waterfront* (an English language film I allowed myself) and I didn't sing, I wasn't a canary. As Rod Steiger said to his younger brother Terry, another Terry, look, kid, you don't say nuttin', you don't see nuttin' and you don't hear nuttin.'

But I had seen and I had read what I had seen. Being the best dressed woman in that factory had done for her. Working in the boss's office and being different from the other women had done for her. She was sexy, she'd got it and she knew she'd got it, and walking in the way she did, walking wavy, with her heels going clack clack clack, walking wavy like Catherine in a *View from the Bridge* had done for her. The heat was rising and some mad bull was banging his head against his cage and he couldn't take it any longer and as he couldn't have her and he couldn't take it any longer he had to hurt her.

Anyway, that was how I read it.

All that early summer, day and night, I was reading American drama in those slim Penguin paperbacks. The slim Greek Penguins had already done their best and their worst with me and now I was into twentieth century drama, the drama of The Common Man, and it was the Americans' turn to click their heels on the sidewalk, to strut their stuff on the world stage, it was their turn to walk wavy.

I couldn't get enough of Tennessee Williams or John Betjeman (strange bedfellows, although perhaps not), and I read them when I was eating a cheese and pickle sandwich or when I was sitting on a wall or during a dead hour in the corner of some stale pub or other. One Sunday afternoon I walked on my own out along the tow-path to Grantchester and sat on a bench in the churchyard there, a very Betjeman scene except I was reading Tennessee Williams, sitting right under the clock tower in fact, reading *A Streetcar Named Desire* it was, and, no, there wasn't honey still for tea, there was no middle-class England on view, there were no Rupert Brooke sonnets and no Betjeman quiz shows on television and there was no skinny dipping in moonlit pools. What there was, was American hysteria.

A Cat on a Hot Tin Roof, *The Rose Tattoo*, *The Glass Menagerie*,

The Night of the Iguana, and *Suddenly Last Summer* (or did that play come later?). Quite apart from the sultry atmosphere and the red meat action, the titles (and *what* titles) were provocation enough. When I had finished all the Tennessee Williams I could get my hands on I planned moving on to Eugene O'Neill and *The Hairy Ape* and *A Long Day's Journey into Night*.

5 | THE TRAGEDY PAPER

In Part 2 of the Cambridge English Tripos there was a tragedy paper. Or, I should say There Was A Tragedy Paper. It was a compulsory part, a central plank, of the examination. You could spend most of your final undergraduate days, and I did, sitting in my rooms or in the college library or the English faculty library or the University Library, reading tragedies, reading tragic plays and tragic novels, or reading the cult critics (say, Raymond Williams and George Steiner) 'on' tragedy, and of course cutting my teeth by being a bit of a critic myself, being a critic of the critics on the critics. Of all this there was no end.

And for reading? There were the Greek fifth century B.C. front runners, Aeschylus and Sophocles; from the first century A.D. there was Seneca and the Romans; then a long jump to the Elizabethans and Jacobeans, to Marlowe, to Shakespeare and Webster and too many others to mention, a hop, skip and jump to France for the eighteenth century tragedians, Racine and Corneille, before heading north for the late nineteenth century Nordic noir of Ibsen and Strindberg, and throw in a great Russian, Chekhov. And, if you felt you needed a break or a different genre, there were the novels of Tolstoy and Dostoyevski. Thomas Hardy, though home-grown and a passable Greek and perfectly tragic enough, did not make the cut.

In the three-hour examination we would be required to

write four essays, in which we would be asked to *discuss* this aspect of tragedy, or to *consider* this aphorism. Whatever the wording, whatever the saying or the paradox, it was tragedy we were unpicking all the way. Tragedy was the supremacy. Life was tragic. Literature was tragic, clearly, particularly tragic.

Yes, in a tragedy there were brief scenes, very brief scenes, which came under the critical heading *comic relief*, without ever tipping over into the actually funny, but they need not detain us for long. I mean, do you ever find yourself slapping your thigh when the Porter is on in *Macbeth*? Yes, I know there's always a mad woman in the audience who does find it funny, every Shakespeare play I go to she starts laughing knowingly at the first pun, Act One Scene One, and there she will always be until the final curtain, usually quite near the front, never missing a tragedy, a history or a comedy. Bet your life she read English at university.

Anyway, the point was there was no comedy paper. In the English faculty there were (that I can remember) no lecture series being offered by a cult don called *In Defence of Comedy*. I'm not sure comedy was intellectually respectable. Instead, my shelves sagged under the full weight – and still do, if I turn round in my seat now I can see the faded hardbacks – of critical studies called *The Harvest of Tragedy, The Story of the Night, Modern Tragedy*, even the most talked about and controversial of them all, George Steiner's 1961 best-seller *The Death of Tragedy*, which began with the paradoxical sentence 'Tragedy is dead.' Not in Cambridge it wasn't. It was alive and kicking, or dead and kicking. My first book, published in the late 1960s when I was teaching and in my mid twenties, was a new critical edition of *King Lear*. The irony was lost on me.

Tragedy, I've had more than enough of it. Now, partly because of John Betjeman, I've settled for History and Comedy.

Early one morning, queasy more from anxiety than from the previous night's beer, I left Terry asleep and walked across to the Senate House. On the walls outside the Senate House there were big wooden display boards on which, day after day, the degree results were pinned. As I took that short walk, my gut liquidising, my stomach clenching, walking from Petty Cury across the Market Square and over King's Parade and into the grounds of the Senate House, I was trying to decide not so much the degree I was expecting to be given let alone the degree I deserved. No, I was asking myself exactly where my eye should land on the list.

When I saw the heading 'English Tripos, Part Two', should I start at the top, searching that tiny group of names (perhaps six names, perhaps ten, they didn't give firsts away in those days) who were awarded first class honours? Or should I, true to my nature, expect a disaster and start down at the bottom, start with the thirds, the lowest class, and then allow my eyes to inch their way modestly, nervously, upwards? Come to think of it, what on earth had this moment been like for Betjeman? He had failed his Oxford degree altogether. His name did not appear.

Well, my eye hit my name straight away, St John's, J.B. Smith. It was not in the very small group at the top, but in the next group down: 2:1, the Upper Seconds, a class satisfyingly smaller, I noticed, than the 2:2 group, the Lower Seconds.

So, a 2:1 it was, then.

The upper part of the second class.

Not brilliant (I wasn't brilliant) but not bad either (I wasn't bad). About right, then. I had worked harder than any of my friends but it was clear that I wasn't that good. Everything that hard work and trying to second-guess the questions (and trying to please the examiners) could do had been done.

Right, so a hard-working-unoriginal-trying-to-please 2:1 it was, then. With my heart settling a little, I then looked for the names of my college friends who also read English, those in my year group, those I went to supervisions or seminars with. (Not lectures, of course: my friends were usually sleeping in, they didn't go to lectures, though I dutifully did.) There was one English scholar in my college, who was brilliant, the one who used the capital R for the lower case r, and he was in the select group, he had got his expected and deserved first. The others in my year did less well than I did. So I came second again. No surprises there.

I walked away from the Senate House, back across the Market Square, past Christ's, up Regent Street, then cut across Parker's Piece with the last of the colleges falling away behind me, with Tennessee Williams, my slim Penguin, in my pocket as I walked towards the factory and the conveyor belt and who knew what lay ahead of me.

Life, I suppose.

My parents, by the way, came up for my graduation day. Clearing out a few drawers recently after our basement was flooded I found a curled up couple of black and white photos of them there, stuck together by the water, a snap of Dad in a dark suit with his trademark white handkerchief in his breast pocket, and there was Mum with her big hat (the agonies she would have gone through choosing that), and me, the centre of attention, leaning back and trying to look casual in my BA hood. I expect they were bursting with pride, and that in itself would have put me off.

I'm ashamed to say I spent as little time with Mum and Dad on my graduation day as I decently could, preferring to be with my close friends, who were of course supposed to be my close friends for the rest of my life, and most of whom I would never clap eyes on again from that day to this.

Once I had settled my two big bills, the books and the

booze, I took Terry out for a few pints of Greene King and a curry and then I hitchhiked back home to Bristol. There was no question of me ever buying a train ticket or a bus ticket to go anywhere. I was a college boy, wasn't I? I was an undergraduate. Well, a graduate now, J.B. Smith Esq B.A, but still a student to all intents and purposes. So I hitchhiked home. We all did. It was so easy. You just stood on a street corner in your jeans or walked out of town for a bit and sat on the dusty roadside verge, looking like the student you were, with or without a long college scarf, and you struck a bored French movie pose and lit a cigarette and raised your languid thumb. Take me or leave me, mate, I'm not begging for anything. We expected drivers to shudder to a halt and back up a bit to where we were sitting and give us a free ride, and God knows why but enough of them did. We were students, weren't we, with long college scarves (not that I wore mine) and we felt entitled, future leaders and all that.

Hard to credit it now. It was a bloody cheek.

Of course I still had no money: no debts but no money either. So I spent the rest of that summer, the summer of 1963, working not in a lemonade factory but on the wide sloping fields of a West Country fruit farm. From the clattering noise of the factory floor I had switched to a very different world, where the quiet warm earth was under my feet as we worked slowly across the fields, row by row by row. My back ached and my pale face and my pale arms were soon burnt nutmeg brown. It was a long, hard day.

There were two other men working shoulder to shoulder with me on those open fields. One was a Polish ex-airman who had stayed on in England after the Second World War, marrying a Bristol girl, and Anglicising his name from Tomasz Wilenski to Tom Williams. After a while I was calling him 'Tennessee', which allusion took a little explaining (Tomasz to Tom to Tennessee) but it seemed to amuse him ('So you say I now change my name again, yes?') and we settled for it.

I could listen to Tomasz talking for hours. He had been through so much; I had been through nothing. As he toiled away with his huge forearms and quick flat fingers he told me about his life in Warsaw and how he got out of there just in time, just before the Nazis moved in: a bit bigger problem than the size of my buttery and books bills. He escaped via Hungary to France to England, and joined one of the Polish squadrons – the legendary 303 squadron – that fought so bravely in the Battle of Britain and elsewhere. My father, who was also in the RAF (as a Pathfinder) in World War Two, told me the Poles were not only very skilful pilots but famously fearless. Never get into a fight with a Pole, my father said.

The other man who worked there was deaf and dumb. At lunch or during our tea breaks, when I was sitting reading under a tree, or (if it was raining) in the hut on the edge of the yard, he would sometimes 'ask' me what I was reading, then gently loosen the paperback from my fingers, his eyes asking the question while he made a low, throaty, guttural sound, and I would nod back at him and say, yes, he's a very good writer. He's American.

'Tennessee Williams,' the Pole would add, pointing to himself and to the Penguin.

7 | BACK ON BETJEMAN

It took a long while, almost a lifetime, before I fully recovered my nerve and got back on the Betjeman horse. No, that's not the right term, not a horse, he had very little time for the horsey world, back on the Betjeman bike is better, back on the Betjeman train.

Ring, ring, toot, toot.

As an undergraduate, and later as a teacher, with Betjeman still on the banned list, my critical eye was trained almost exclusively on 'difficulty', on difficult poets, on wrestling with puzzling poets, on writers who never held your hand. It was John Donne not Joan Hunter Dunn, it was Gerard Manley Hopkins not Archibald Ormsby-Gore, it was all T.S. Eliot, T.E. Hulme and Ezra Pound (and I had not a mortal clue what was going on). I was aware of their many qualities and distinctions, of course I was, and amongst educated people I found a passably intelligent way of talking about their works, but, to be frank, I often hadn't 'got' any of them. And if I didn't understand the poems or felt intellectually lost I kept very quiet about it, hoping to be unnoticed, while allowing it to be thought that I did understand. After craven decades of this, when I found I was...

Nearly fifty summers older,
Richer, wickeder and colder

... a friend, quite out of the blue in the 1990s, gave me as a birthday present the *Collected Poems of John Betjeman*.

At first I did not open the book, beyond reading the birthday inscription and having the occasional glance at my over-crowded shelves to see if it was still there. It was as if Betjeman was still my guilty secret, a writer of light verse, a poetic skeleton in my intellectual cupboard, an academic stain, and here was an unwelcome reminder of those distant days when I did not know my major from my minor.

Then – for God's sake get a grip, Jonathan, grow up, you know you want a drink, you know you do, deep down you know you like him, so I reached out and picked the book up, picked him up, took him down, poured myself a decent drink and started to read his poems from the beginning, which means starting, as they say, from page one.

While reading the third poem, on page five, I felt the first jolt. It was the third verse in *The Varsity Students' Rag*, a very early poem of his, and it went, it goes like this:

But that's nothing to the rag we had at the college the other night;
We'd gallons and gallons of cider – and I got frightfully tight.
And then we smash'd up ev'rything, and what was the funniest
  part
We smashed some rotten old pictures which were priceless works
  of art.

And, bang goes the Bullingdon Club, there were the entitled Bullingdon Boys, nailed for all time. Two pages later, on page seven, I came across *The City*:

Business men with awkward hips
And dirty jokes upon their lips,
And large behinds and jingling chains,
And riddled teeth and riddling brains,
And plump white fingers made to curl
Round some anaemic city girl,
And so lend colour to the lives
And old suspicions of their wives.

Young men who wear on office stools
The ties of minor public schools,
Each learning how to be a sinner
And tell 'a good one' after dinner…

And, after reading all the *Collected Poems*, including *Summoned by Bells*, circling or ticking some titles, making approving pencil marks or comments in the margin, I went back to the beginning, back to *Death in Leamington*, and started them all over again. This time they seemed different, darker, stronger, subtly, significantly different. They also, importantly, seemed more important. There were echoes of Hardy and that bit is Larkin, I said to myself, well before Larkin was writing, and, more surprisingly, that's Eliot.

Larkin, Eliot.

Larkin hugely rated Betjeman.

Eliot wanted to publish Betjeman.

I widened my focus. So much for his work, what about his life? I set off on the big three-volume biography by Bevis Hillier, a treasure trove, and then the two volumes of Betjeman's selected letters (edited by his daughter, Candida, wonderfully edited), and a collection of his prose pieces. I read the A.N. Wilson biography. I read and read, in a world of my own, or his own, yes, such was the immersion I was leaving mine and moving into his. Betjeman was now a permanent and open thread in my life, his life in mine, my life in his. Friends, the kinder ones, a touch wearily, a touch warily, sometimes asked me

–Are you still on Betjeman?

–I am.

–You don't think it's time for a break?

–No.

–Not stuck, are you?

I never enjoy these questions, these probing moments.

–No.

–So what are you up to?

–Not sure.

And I'm still not sure, and that's partly why I'm writing this book. Two things, however, struck me. Betjeman was not the writer he was popularly thought to be. Or not simply. The popular bit was there all right, which I applaud because what on earth is wrong with being popular? I'd like to be popular, and preferably before I die; I'd like to be a household name, how about today but tomorrow will do. And which writer in any genre – above all which poet – wouldn't like to sell over two million copies? It's surely better than selling seven copies, all signed. I was asked, only once (and there'll never, I assure you, be a second time), asked by a big bookshop (all right, Waterstones) to do a signing and I said yes and I stood there for two hours looking a right Charley and sold one copy, and that was to a friend who I rang up from the shop and asked to get down there sharpish.

Or is Betjeman's popularity as grave a critical sin as his accessibility, a critical crime akin to clarity? At a literary launch a few years back I asked someone I was standing next to what he thought of Seamus Heaney's latest collection, which I admired, and he said, with the smallest and tightest of smiles, 'Famous Shaymus? Oh, very ac-cess-ible, isn't he?' and I wanted to say oh do fuck off but I couldn't muster the energy. It was a re-run of my undergraduate days, still going on, all of it, still going on.

Anyway.

What about Betjeman's little known poems, the poems of his that very few people ever mention? Have they even been read, or do they not neatly tie in with the popular image in the minds of his fans and his detractors?

What about *Devonshire Street, WI*, that magnificent poem set in a doctor's consulting rooms (and surely you hear Larkin):

The heavy mahogany door with its wrought-iron screen
Shuts. And the sound is rich, sympathetic, discreet.
The sun still shines on this eighteenth century scene
With Edwardian faience adornments – Devonshire Street.

No hope. And the X-ray photographs under his arm
Confirm the message. His wife stands timidly by.

The opposite brick-built house looks lofty and calm
Its chimneys steady against a mackerel sky.

No hope. And the iron nob of this palisade
So cold to the touch, is luckier now than he.
'Oh merciless, hurrying Londoners! Why was I made
For the long and the painful deathbed coming to me?'

She puts her fingers in his as, loving and silly,
At long-past Kensington dances she used to do
'It's cheaper to take the tube to Piccadilly
And then we catch a nineteen or a twenty-two.'

8 | HOW TO TELL THE STORY

Having fallen yet again – and this time finally – under Betjeman's spell, I could not decide how to tell the story I wanted to write. And how to tell the story is such a fundamental, yet such a tricky, issue, and indeed a trickiness which was later compounded by my illness which brought about a collapse in my confidence.

Was I up to it? Was I up for it, and, if so, which form, which genre, does this narrative suit? Should it be a novel? A writer friend suggested to me that it should, she was quite sure, it's a confessional novel all right, she said, and it's right up your street, Jonathan. Oh, too kind, too kind. *And there is something very pleasant, old boy*, as Betjeman wrote to Cyril Connolly, *about seeing one's own name in print.*

Or would it make a better script for television? But the issue is, does Betjeman *resonate* with today's audience, and those in television do love things to resonate. Sorry to say this, they say *sotto voce*, but isn't he, as he himself often feared he was, a bit trivial and out of date? No, wrong, wrong, wrong. Or perhaps it's a stage play? Difficult one, that. Or does it make most sense as voices for radio? It does.

I've got it, why not just write a book?

Or, radio *and* a book.

In the early stages of writing something new I usually go through these periods of doubt and uncertainty, these internal writhings, during which I leave sticky yellow notes for myself in my hut, with clear instructions such as *Do Stop Arsing About*, or in which I echo the timeless advice shouted at a cricket match by a fat spectator at a becalmed batsman who is stubbornly occupying the crease but scoring no runs, *Get On With It*.

The trouble with such self-flagellation, even when you are well, is that you can then browbeat yourself into producing something superficially skilful but contrived, something factitious, filling pages and pages with writing which may be professionally tolerable but which is not in your own voice: pages that don't ring true. My most prolonged and 'expensive' error was writing a whole novel in the first person before deciding, after a final read-through, that something was wrong and it would work much better in the more conventional third.

It's not unusual for me to write 'it', the story, as a play then switch to a novel, or – as I did with the Betjeman radio plays – to write the scenes as chapters in a novel and then to adapt them into plays. And here, in this book, I am using the novel narrative form because I don't find setting it out as play dialogue so easy on the eye, or so welcoming, or so easy to live with. In fact, to be honest, I'm turned off by novels which suddenly switch into play format.

But whichever way round it is, novel or play or fusion, off I go, galloping ahead full of energy on this tack, before jumping horses, trying one, then trying the other, on a creative whim or breeze, falling at fences, and sometimes limping home in a defeated mood, only to get up the next morning saying I'm buggered if I'm going to be beaten. In a generously forgiving mood you could call this a form of resilience, you could see this as a sign of a tough guy, but it feels more like a nasty mixture of stubbornness and pride. It's small comfort, very small comfort, to remind myself that Wordsworth knew all about these false dawns, faffing around on the fells and finding it hard to settle to his theme, before hitting his stride with his autobiographical 'spots of time' in *The Prelude*.

At least I know where to start. I'm starting in 1928. I'm going to begin with Betjeman, aged 22, having left Oxford. I'm starting with him getting on a train at Waterloo, getting on the Cornish Riviera Express. That works if it's a novel. If I do it as a play and kick off with him leaving Oxford, I think I'll need to create two Betjemans, The Younger Adult Betjeman and The Older Betjeman. But that's all right, my older and younger selves already co-exist: whatever age I may look in the mirror, I am still young inside, or feel so, indeed I have accepted I am many selves inside. Aren't we all?

9 | THE ATLANTIC COAST EXPRESS, 1928

The Old Great Western Railway shakes
The Old Great Western Railway spins,
The Old Great Western Railway makes
Me very sorry for my sins.

He made the train, just.

He sat back in his seat, hot and clammy, slowly recovering his breath as the whistle blew.

Leaving Waterloo at 10.35 in the morning, with a

luncheon car attached, the Atlantic Coast Express curved her way south-westwards across the heart of the country, rolling over the downs and the plains, calling at Salisbury (12.01) and Exeter St David's (1.41), then steaming on through broad red Devon before she crossed into Cornwall and, around tea time, pulled into her final destination on the Camel estuary, the fishing port of Padstow.

Normally it was a journey he loved. Every station the train called at – from the grandest one designed by Isambard Kingdom Brunel to the most modest of rural halts – was as familiar to him as the back of his hand. It was a trip he had taken so many times he knew every incline and bend in the track, every hill and river they passed, every town and tor.

While other passengers talked or read the daily papers or fell into a doze, he leant forward and smoked a Turkish cigarette, a Balkan Sobranie. His eye took in the ever-changing landscape of England. His eye picked up precise mundane details, the most everyday of details, with no detail too small. Or, with a sudden burst of restless energy, he would turn away from the window to grab a piece of notepaper and write a letter – often scurrilous and decorated with drawings – to a dear friend. Or he might start a poem, jotting down a phrase here, playing with a rhyme there, and he might come up with something, perhaps along the lines of,

> *The Old Great Western Railway shakes*
> *The Old Great Western Railway spins,*

And then, after skirting the granite edges of Bodmin Moor, he would normally step down onto the platform at Wadebridge station, at 4.10 or thereabouts, taking in the salty scents and the familiar trees until, soon coming into view, he saw again the unaltered cliffs and the sight of elderly schoolmasters in shorts.

But today was not normal. Today was quite different. On the final leg of the journey, from Launceston and Camelford, with the train emptying, he was increasingly fidgety and churned up. Famous though he was for staving things off, this was one he could stave off no longer. He could not settle because he had been forced to accept that he had no choice, no sniff of a choice, but to go down to Cornwall, to the tiny village of Trebetherick, and tell his parents. Well, tell *him* really. She would be fine, his dear mother, his dear old Bessie would be fine, but that was scant comfort because, truth to tell, when it came to anything serious she did not count.

As for his father… at that thought, at that picture, he closed his eyes and slowly shook his head. As for Ernest Betjemann, he was another matter altogether. Not that he would ever dream of calling his father Ernest to his face, let alone Ernie. Perish the thought. That liberty, that sardonic belittling familiarity, was reserved for his disloyal letters to his dearest friends.

He put away his pen.

There was a Big Talking To in the pipeline.

No doubt about it. Big.

How he wished he were dead.

Or ill in bed with frostbite.

Whatever scrap of evidence was adduced in his son's defence, his father did not understand and his father would never understand, because Ernie Betjemann had not gone to university. Ernie Betjemann did not know the first thing about undergraduate life, nor care much for varsity rags and getting drunk and trashing people's rooms. He had no truck with the Bullingdon boys or similar societies. What he did know about was business and the bottom line and factory floors and Bond Street, business and bills and Pentonville Road and trade. And, with the aid of his large ear trumpet, he would soon become aware of his son's latest news.

The light was just beginning to go as John turned the sharp

left-hand corner at the top of Daymer Lane. Nearly there. He passed the white-washed post office, and slowly, ever more slowly, his feet dropped down towards the water's edge and the sands, the sands on which he had diverted many a stream and planned many a dam. To the left of the beach lay the dunes and St Enodoc church and the golf course, though these could not be spotted from the steep, high-banked lane. Every driveway and lawn he passed was as well kept as they always had been, and as he walked on down he could hear coming from behind the line of conifers the sound of girls' voices and the plonk and thwack of tennis balls.

With their house – their holiday home, though it felt far more than that – coming up round the next bend, he stopped in the middle of the road. And took stock. He had given them no prior warning. He had not written a letter or made a telephone call. Instead, he had decided he would turn up unannounced, with a dash of devil-may-care drama, and take whatever came on the chin. What had, however, seemed a brave intention in Chelsea became mere bravado in the clear cold light of Cornwall.

Again, having moved on, he slowed in his tracks, taking some deep breaths, to dissipate or at least to lessen his fears. He counted up to ten. *Un, deux, trois… Courage, mes enfants.* He could now faintly hear the lap of the ocean, and he could see a light in their kitchen, and he was hoping against hope that his dear mother with her welcoming warmth and a whacking great kiss would be the one to lift the latch.

His father, however, was standing there. His father, a picture of health, was filling the front door frame. His father, with his egg-shaped head, central parting and moustache, stance bolt upright, his pipe smouldering in his palm, and with his tobacco smell as sweet and permeating as ever.

He stared hard at his son, checking him from unkempt top to unpolished toe.

'Isn't it term time?'

'Yes, Father, it is.'

'What?'

'I said yes, Father. It is term time.'

'Well, whatever brings you here, you'd better come in.'

Without looking round to see if she was there, he shouted over his shoulder, 'Bessie! Bessie, look who's here!'

'John! It's John. John, John, John, what a lovely surprise!'

'Come through, boy.'

He followed his father, head down, into the sitting room, with his mother pressing hard on his heels, and there he had to turn and face them, face him rather, and deliver the news of his disgrace. This he announced into the ebony mouthpiece of his father's ear trumpet, the trumpet which all three of them liked to pretend did not exist.

Ernest Betjemann had no time for lip reading or any nonsense of that sort, and when he spoke it was always with the volume knob on full.

'Didn't hear you.'

'I said I've been sent down.'

'Sent down?'

'Yes.'

'Does that mean sacked?'

'Yes, it does.'

'You've been sacked from Oxford?'

'I have.'

'Expelled from the university without a degree of any kind what-so-ever?'

'Yes, I have. But, by the way, and not that it matters, you're *expelled* from a school, but you're *sent down* from university.'

'Is that so?'

'Yes. Technically.'

'I do not,' Ernest Betjemann boomed, 'require a lecture from you on my use of language, not at this par-tic-u-lar *junc*-ture. Thank you.'

'Sorry, Father.'

'Dressed up as a girl again, were you?'

'No!'

'Drunk and disorderly?'

'No, I failed my examinations.'

'Oh, you poor poor boy,' his mother said. 'The brutes.'

'I thought you were meant to be intelligent.'

'I am intelligent!' he flared back.

'You are?'

'Yes, very intelligent. But no one at Magdalen lifted a finger to help me.'

'No one?'

'No, not even C.S. Lewis. Above all, C.S. Lewis.'

'Who is C.S. Lewis?'

'My tutor.'

'Never heard of him. What does he do?'

'I've just told you, haven't I, he's my tutor. That is, he teaches me. Well, taught me, rather. After his fashion. And he's the one who could have saved me, easily, if he'd cared to.'

'But he didn't care to?'

'No. No, he didn't.'

'And why didn't he care to?'

'Be-cause, because he hates me, because he always has hated me. And don't ask me why. Who knows what makes A hate B? But there's always been bad blood between us. He's from Belfast.'

'So you also fell out with the most important person in the college?'

'He's not that important.'

'Isn't he?'

'No, he just thinks he is.'

'Thinks he is?'

'Thinks he's a writer as well, and he isn't, he's beta plus at

37

best and a bit of a bore, but he's been my undoing, ghastly man.'

His father strode to the fireplace, bent down and grabbed the poker. As he roughly turned over the logs and rearranged the lumps of coal, he stirred up a strong sooty smell.

'No, John, he hasn't been your undoing, your character's been your undoing. As it always has been. This has been coming for years. With your arrogance, and your superior ways, not to mention all this fooling about with pansies.'

'Pansies?'

'What would you call them?'

'Friends.'

'Friends!'

'Yes, friends.'

'Funny sort of friends, neither fish nor fowl, and look where they have landed you. But then you've never been a good judge of people.'

John tried to swallow. His mouth was parched and his nostrils twitched with the soot and his ears burnt (and would be burning for months, if not years, as he re-played this scene of shame), having to spell out the ignominy, having to suffer the humiliation, to eat the humble family pie, and then, knowing only too well it was on its way, seeing the storm coming across the estuary, here we go, any minute now, he would be having to listen yet again to –

'All that money I spent on you, sending you to Marl-bor-ough, all that priv-i-lege, for *what*? To fritter your life away!'

Knowing it was coming, John did his level best to tune it out as noise, nothing more and nothing less, noise, and also, if possible, to ignore Ernie's predictable and lifelong mispronunciations. The trick was to let everything pass over your head, let the old man say what he likes in any straight-shooting way of his choice. Let him bang on to his heart's content and get it off his chest. Besides, you have no option, you're in no position to do a damned thing, so you'll just have to stand here, won't you, and hear him out.

The point was, it was all over. He had thrown away Oxford, a pearl of precious price. He had packed his Oxford bags and said his sad goodbyes and walked away for the last time from the mellow walls and the wide-sashed windows of Magdalen. He was out on his inglorious ear, and whatever his mother might keep on asserting there was no going back: there was to be no more fun, no more excess, there would be no more sallies of wit, no more rakish cars and long country house weekends. True, he hadn't done any academic work, but then who had? True, he had misbehaved, but then who hadn't?

Meanwhile, his mother was trying to get a word in edgeways:

'They'll have you back next year, John dear. You'll see. Once they realise the terrible mistake they've made. Mark my words, just mark my words. Oh, no,' she clasped her hand to her jaw, 'I knew it, I knew it, it's set off my toothache.'

As he always had done, Ernie ignored his wife's toothache. He was into his stride. He was hitting his straps.

'All that money down the drain, but no surprises there. Huge fees spent on my son and heir. On my only child. Not what you'd call a solid in-*vest*-ment, my boy, are you? And it's not difficult to see the reason, it's as plain as the nose on your face. Because you are bone lazy. Not content with changing the family name, without a hint of a by-your-leave, you now go and get yourself sacked. I should have known. Change the spelling of your family name, a respected name up and down Bond Street, and not even discuss it with me!'

'You know why he did that, dear. They thought he was German.'

Ernie ignored this too, the Germans joining the tooth-aches. Tiny bubbles of spittle were beginning to multiply at the corners of his mouth.

'Four generations of Betjemanns, that's what we are: a proud firm with a proud name. And, what do you do, you go and change the spelling! I knew there was trouble ahead when I heard what you'd done, because it's the sort of thing a second-rate chap would do.'

'I think that's a little unfair, dear, when –

'And what about the firm?'

'The firm?'

'Who's going to run the factory after me? Eh? Eh? And I'll tell you something else. *We* Betjemanns don't get sacked. And I'll tell you why. We don't get sacked because *we sack other people.*'

At which point his father crossed the room, his face fast shut, his feet hitting the carpet hard, saying,

'I'm going out.'

'Don't go too far, dear, will you.'

'What!'

'I said, don't go too far, it's nearly dark.'

'Well, I can see that, can't I! I'm not blind. And at least one thing in this whole mess is clear. Crystal clear. But in case there can be any doubt let me spell it out. To both of you. This episode, this disgraceful episode, marks the end of your allowance. Do not look to me ever again for any financial assistance. You are on your own, and let's see how you do. You're a rotten, low, deceitful little snob.'

As the front door banged behind his father, his mother sighed a long sigh and smiled the cosiest of smiles at her son,

'Never mind, John darling. He'll feel better when he's biffed a few golf balls.'

10 | St Enodoc churchyard, 1928

He awoke to a dawn of guilt and a day of short tempers. He pulled on his clothes and unhooked a smelly mackintosh from the coat stand in the hall and was down the lane and stepping on to the beach well before the first dog.

Head down, without even looking out to sea, he cut through the dunes towards the church, crossed the fairway and circled the edge of the green, before hurrying on up through the graveyard so that he could sit where he always sat, in his seat, his seat and no one else's seat, alone in the tilting rain.

Here, in sight but just too far for the roar of the sea, he covered his face with his hands. Behind him a thoughtless blackbird chose that very moment to start singing.

His conduct had, without a doubt, been reprehensible and he would be left to burn. He cursed himself. You are an idiot, he said. You are a bloody idiot, he said. In point of fact, he continued, you are a complete and utter fucking idiot. Then, with that acknowledgement out of the way, he dropped his hands and opened his eyes and, for the first time that morning, watched the ocean flinging up its spume against the cliffs.

Sitting alone on that wooden bench at the highest point of St Enodoc churchyard, as he liked to do even in a slamming gale, with his back to the lichened wall, he had it all laid out before him like an opera set. And, come to think of it, his life at the moment was a bit like an opera. A bad opera.

The sacred ground, tightly packed with tombstones, fell sharply away beneath his feet, which were on the same level as the roof of the nave. He looked westwards over the roof and the crooked spire to Brae Hill, and beyond that to the wide backcloth of the Atlantic Ocean. Straight ahead, lying between the dunes and the sea, was Daymer Bay, a wide and safe stretch of sand on which he had always peered into rock pools and where he often had been the butterfingers who dropped the vital catch.

To his left was the St Enodoc Golf Course, the course on which his father always played his round come rain or shine. Just below the church lay the 10th green, as immaculate as all the other greens on the links.

Further to his left was the Camel Estuary and the ferry from Rock across to Padstow. How he had loved that ferry as a child, and he still did. A short crossing it may be, barely ten minutes at most, but however cold and choppy the water it never failed to warm his heart and lift his spirits. Who knows, perhaps a crossing on the ferry and a meander around the narrow streets of Padstow would (even today) cheer him up.

As a schoolboy, as well as an undergraduate, he often came to sit here in this churchyard, and it never failed to settle him down and give him comfort, a safe spot in a turning world. Thank God it was always there, this seat, this place and this view, but he had never felt more uncomfortable, his life never more out of tune than it did on that wet morning.

Feeling remorse and feeling small, he drifted down the steep slope and opened the door into the tiny, unlocked church, the church where every Sunday his family had worshipped together, every Sunday since he was knee-high to a grass-hopper, since the time when he liked to bump his face into his father's tweeds, and where, once he was confirmed, the three of them went up, father, mother and son, kneeling side by side together, to take Holy Communion.

He stopped. He stood, contrite, just inside the door and looked around the church. Everything was as it was and as it should be. It was as if he were soberly greeting old friends, nodding imperceptibly at each and every one in recognition: the Norman font, the screen, the chancel, the pulpit, the vestry, the lancet window. Still there, always there.

He took a few paces up the aisle and slipped into the Betjemann family pew. He glanced up at the altar and the east window, and then dropped to his knees.

Dear Lord

Please, God!

But, screw his eyes up tight and try as hard as he could, so insistent were the other voices in his head he could not pray. Prayer was a lost cause. Which was not the hardest thing to work out because, this morning, that's what he was himself, a lost cause. He briskly asked God for forgiveness and came up off his knees, determined to be a man and to stop feeling sorry for himself. He had to become a man, and a man must take stock.

It was time to give himself A Talking To.

A Talking To every bit as harsh as his father's.

He was twenty-two. Fact.

He had failed at Oxford. Fact.

He had let himself and his family down. He'd made a botch of it. So, aged twenty-two, he was down on his uppers, no doubt about it, with no allowance from his father, ay, there's the rub: Ernie Betjemann was nothing if not an adamant man and Ernie Betjemann would stick to his guns.

So, he had no money forthcoming, and he had big debts.

What did he do?

What could he do?

So, there and then, sitting slouched in the family pew in that small Cornish church, he decided that he would go straight back to London, straight back to Waterloo on the Atlantic Coast Express, and do what anyone does who has no qualifications and cannot get a job: he would teach at a prep school. Someone somewhere would, and for the usual reason, have been quietly moved on. A vacancy would occur. A job of sorts would need doing. Somewhere in that barking world a headmaster would want him.

Surely?

11 | LANDING A JOB, 1928

A nd so it proved. There was such a school. There was such a vacancy. After a week or two of rejections, a letter arrived in which he was offered a temporary post as master-in-charge of cricket, with a bit of English on the side, at one hundred and eighty pounds a year, no questions asked, all found. There was no formal interview or anything silly like that, though the headmaster did take some notes at the end of their first meeting, which he kept in the bottom drawer of his desk:

Betjeman

Odd-looking cove, probably from a small claque.

Protruding teeth, dazzling pullover and canary yellow tie, the sort unstable people wear.

Manner rather cavalier and disrespectful. To put it mildly, some of his answers were in the wrong key.

Too much hermaphrodite laughter for my taste.

More charitably, might just have been nerves.

May be problems ahead? Not sure the anchor would hold in a storm.

Could be good.

Mind you, there was a potential hitch, which John had not brought up with the headmaster and one that he felt might prove troublesome, if not a stumbling block. He did not know one end of a cricket bat from the other. He would be on the field under false pretences, an interloper. He saw it coming:

'Decent at games, are you?' the headmaster had asked.

'Passably... decent, I'd say.'

'Cricket?'

'Rath-er.'

'Good, good. And how's your English?'

'Oh, coming on. Most of the time I get away with it.'

He'd only ever played the wretched game of cricket once, properly that is, with pads and gloves and a hard ball, and as luck would have it he was hit in what they call the box area, the testes, unprotected and flush on, and as he explained to the girls who had no personal knowledge of this sort of thing, it was jolly painful.

On hearing through his ear trumpet the terms of his son's employment, Ernie Betjemann was incredulous:

'*You?* Master in charge of cricket?'

'Yes.'

'*Crick-et?*'

'Yes.'

'At a pre-par-a-tory school no one has ever heard of!'

'Yes.'

'It's not exactly your Eton or Harrow, then?'

'Eton and Harrow are not prep schools. They are public schools.'

'Whatever it is, where is it?'

'In Cockfosters, father.'

'Didn't hear you!'

'*Cock-fos-ters!* On the *Picc-a-dilly* Line.'

12 | WHERE DID IT ALL GO WRONG?

Who knows when and where it all starts to go wrong between parents and children? The winds, as Auden says, must come from somewhere when they blow. Because it begins so well, doesn't it? A birth sets one singing. That is only natural. The newborn child captivates the parents' hearts.

Presumably, then, the 28th of August 1906 was a fine summer's day for Ernest and Mabel Bessie Betjemann, that baby-proud moment when their boy arrived in the world, or, to be exact, in 52 Parliament Hill Mansions, London. There was his upright, proud father leaning stiffly over the crib which held his son, the son who would one fine day take over the firm. Betjemann and Sons.

Then there was his mother cooing over baby's first smile, then marvelling at his first wobbly steps and his first wobbly tooth. Bumps, tears, his first bruise, there-there, come to Mumsie. How happy all that must have been, that North London nursery world, that geography of hope, with everything all starchy and tickety-boo.

This is my son, mine own Telemachus,
To whom I leave the sceptre and the isle.

So, what started the slow slide to the child John being a little duffer with protruding teeth, *you little duffer, John*, then sliding more quickly into being a little clown and then into an exhibitionist before settling down as a steadily disloyal son who deeply grieved his father? What caused the first crack in the glass? When did contempt take over from frustration? Do you, as Betjeman asks himself, bury your differences or do you thrash them out? Not an easy one to answer.

There's the salutary father and son story of Dr Johnson. It's in Boswell. Boswell tells us that Dr Johnson stood bare-headed in the driving rain in Uttoxeter market, like King Lear out in the storm, allowing the heavy rain to beat down on his bare head, to expiate the painful memory of snubbing his father who, many decades earlier, had appealed to him to tend his bookstall there. And the young Johnson, out of pride, had refused. For Dr Johnson in his later years it was a time for penance, a time to stand bare-headed in the rain. Pour on.

Pride, ingratitude, snobbery, the harsh patronage of youth and the gratification of anger, they are all in the mix.

Or take Shelley. He was enraged, so enraged by the narrow-mindedness and materialism of his blameless father that at one point he contemplated murdering him. Or so a scholarly friend in Worcestershire tells me.

13 | A HOPELESS DAWN, 1916

Things were not always bad between John and his father, not in the beginning. Far from it. In their Highgate days, at number 31 West Hill, they were the suburban middle class, well settled among the well-off in Middlesex, and it was that time of his young life when a piggy-back from his father was something to look forward to, an evening treat, with his bristly face and his Adam's apple sharp on his son's arm.

'Up on my back, boy, up you get, on my shoulders, then up we go, up, up the wooden stairs.'

'Gee up, Daddy.'

'It's quite steep for a piggy-back, Ernest.'

'Don't fuss the boy, Bessie, or he'll be dancing with the daffodils.'

And up the first flight they went at a gallop. What long strides his father took! How springy his step!

'Be careful on the corner, Ernest.'

'Grip me tightly, boy. Tight-er! You feel like a girl.'

Bessie was bringing up the rear, struggling to keep in touch, panting heavily, calling out:

'And remember, clean your teeth, John dear. Twenty brushes, top and bottom.'

Ernest missed all of this. He heard not a word of his wife's, and was content with that.

'That's it, let me feel your muscles. And tomorrow we'll do some catching practice. And soon you'll be a big boy. Away at school. At Marl-bor-ough. With new chums. Think of that!'

He took me on long silent walks
In country lanes when young,
He knew the name of ev'ry bird,
But not the song it sung.

Later that holiday, he took John, it was just the two of them, to the Tate Gallery to see the Cornish paintings, to see the Newlyn painters. Sportsman though he was, his father liked to paint a bit himself when he could get time away from the factory, oils mainly, some watercolours, and they weren't at all bad even if he said so himself, seascapes, rocks, cliff tops, sunsets, Cornwall, that sort of caper. No people.

Ernest strode impatiently through the rooms of the gallery, talking loudly as he did so:

'Can't you smell the spray! Shoulders back, boy. Shoulder blades together. Head up. No, straighter than that. That's it! Chest out. Don't cower. Before long we'll be playing golf together down at St Enodoc. The best course in Cornwall. A real test for both of us, some tricky holes there, let me tell you.'

But the boy could not stop staring at the human exhibits, the missing legs, the pasty faces, the crutches, the missing hands, the gallery half full of wounded soldiers back from the Front. Then, two paintings away, there was a woman in a dress of green sheen. Why did his mother never dress like that?

'Look at the *paintings*, boy. Manners.'

'Sorry, Father.'

'And you'll enjoy the Norfolk Broads this summer. More than your mother does. East Anglian light, very different from the West. We'll go there, the two of us. Eh? Chaps together.'

*

The very next week they returned, chaps together, to the Tate for a second visit, his father once again marching ahead.

'John!' he barked.

'Yes, Father.'

'This is the one. Quickly!'

'Coming.'

'It's a very famous painting.'

'Is it?'

'Meant to show it you last week. Almost as popular as *And When Did You Last See Your Father.*'

His father couldn't do anything about it, John realised that, he couldn't help it at all, but if only he would not speak *quite* so loudly. People would look. Indeed, two men in uniform *were* looking at him, one soldier in particular, the one with the mark on his face. And that woman was there again, the same woman, in her dress of green sheen, she was looking at him too, her eyes floating their way.

His father's hearing impediment, coupled with his inability to control the volume of his voice, was a daily embarrassment for the boy. An art gallery, even when as crowded as the Tate, was at its heart a quiet place. An art gallery was a small palace of attentive whispers, an atmosphere in which people put their heads privately together and leant forward to discuss in detail the pictures on the walls. A hushed art gallery was, John noticed, akin to a fine parish church, if not on its way to being a small cathedral.

'Where do you think it is set, John?'

The boy gawped, and his jaw dropped. It was a habit of his to stare, eyes wide, with his mouth staying open.

'Don't catch flies, boy.'

Ernest always said that, don't catch flies, when he saw his son's mouth gape.

'Could it be Cornwall, Father?'

'Well, they're *all* Cornwall, dimwit. Tell me something new.'

But the boy's eyes were too busy reading the picture to register the insult. His eyes were moving so quickly his mind was unable to order itself into sentences.

'Who painted it, boy?' his father asked.

The boy moved closer to the painting and read out,

'Frank Bramley. 1888. Oil on canvas.'

'And his dates?'

'1857–1915. So he died last year?'

'We all have to die sometime, John.'

'But not fighting the Germans?'

'No, not in battle. You like it? Do you like it?'

'It's the best picture I've ever seen.'

His words just bubbled out of him, unbidden, and his father smiled, a rare enough event on any day.

'And what's the *story*, eh? In life there's always a story, remember that.'

If only his father would move a little closer to the painting, then they would run less risk of being the centre of unwelcome attention.

'Oh, come on.'

The father stood stock still in his grey suit, towering over his son. He tapped his foot a few times.

'The title is a clue.'

His father's foot was tapping more loudly.

'In my experience, John, when people do not state the obvious it is usually because they haven't spotted it. What is the painting called, boy?'

'*A Hopeless Dawn.*'

John had known without being told that the scene was tragic and he loved tragedy because tragedy attracted attention. Painted on the canvas before him there was a dark interior, a dark low room in a small cottage. Outside, through the window, a storm was raging, a storm that makes trees roar and bend landwards, a big sea, like a rough day off Trebetherick, like Doom Bar with crashing white breakers. Inside the dark room, on the right-hand side of the painting, an older woman and a younger woman were desperately holding on to each other, clinging together, rather as he did at night with Archie.

The boy loved pictures that told a story, and the bigger the story the better. The Crucifixion was, of course, the biggest story of them all. So, what was the story between these two women? The older woman appeared to be comforting the younger one, who was burying her head as if unable to face the day. If this was dawn, had they been awake all night?

'What are they doing, the women?'

'Father.'

'What?'

'Could you speak a little more quietly, please?'

'What?'

He gave up and turned back to the canvas. No, stupid, no, it's obvious, a man, a fisherman, has been lost at sea. A husband had been dashed on a rock. A son had been rolled in the surf.

'Can I stay? Please.'

His father looked at him with suspicion.

'Here? You want to stay here?'

'I do.'

'Are you writing one of your poems?'

'I might be.'

'You *might be*. Is that your devious way of saying you are?'

'It might be.'

His father roared with laughter, and this time his son did not mind the volume of the noise and the attention it brought. He liked making people laugh, he could do it, he liked being witty, in class he often chose to be the clown, and causing his father to laugh was special. At that moment, towering above him in his pale grey suit, there was an admiring radiance about his father, and his whiskers were resplendent.

'Make sure you are here, boy, when I come back. Don't go wandering off anywhere.'

'I won't.'

'I don't want your mother saying I've lost you. She'd never stop. As it is she worries herself sick over the slightest trifle, as you may have noticed. For example, this morning, your coat being buttoned up wrongly. And the wrong marmalade at breakfast can cause a splitting headache or a troublesome tooth. She's a martyr to her toothache.'

'I am not going anywhere, Father.'

What a day this was proving to be! His father had never before spoken to him about his mother like that, about buttoned up coats and marmalade and troublesome teeth, and certainly not in that tone. This was the longest speech he had ever heard on such a topic. And it was spoken as if they were equals, as if there was something new and understood between them, as if an iron-studded church door had (without the boy pushing it) suddenly swung open.

That very morning, from the doorway to the bathroom, John had watched his father shaving, his long bony fingers holding up his cut throat razor in front of the steamed up mirror, occasionally wiping the mirror with his elbow before scraping the blade around his mouth, carefully avoiding his moustache, then scraping his cheeks, his chin, his neck, dipping his razor slowly and deliberately in the hot soapy water. From the doorway the boy could see the foam tide around the rim of the basin was flecked with tiny dark hairs, and he could hear the rough drag of the blade on his father's skin and his nostrils breathing heavily. His father knew his boy was there, close to him, and he allowed him to watch.

And here, in the gallery, his father was again indulging him. At that moment he loved his father so much his soul soared up. His stern father had taken his part and for all John minded his father could have picked him up and held him tight in front of the whole gallery, even in front of the men in uniform, with all their eyes turned their way, and the boy would not have been embarrassed.

The depth of the tender joy he felt for his deaf father as he stood before that painting in that gallery was matched only by the bewildering depth of his anger with him in later years, and the anger at himself for the way he had allowed himself to be dragged down like a deadweight into flailing annoyance and censorious contempt.

Bwt, despite those days shared in the gallery, Ernest Betjemann had seen enough, enough in Cornwall and enough on the Norfolk Broads, more than enough of his son anywhere near a golf club or a gun or a cricket ball, and when Ernest Betjemann's tune changed it changed for ever.

'I'd get used to your own company, boy, because I can't see any sporting fellows wanting you to join them. You'll be unpopular at Marl-bor-ough if you can't catch a ball. Here. Now, we'll try again, this time with a tennis ball, even if it is a girl's game. It should be soft enough for you. Ready? Fingers spread. Eyes on the ball. Read-y? Oh, *catch* it, can't you!'

He gave up. He threw up his hands. He may or may not have muttered the word 'drip' but that is what the boy was. A drip. He plonked the basket of balls back under the stairs and walked away, his sporting heart broken. On his next attendance at church he would have prayed, and prayed very hard, as only a sporty middle-class English father can, that his son would not let him down on the games field.

But most of all he hated finding the boy in bed with Archie. John loved Archibald Ormsby-Gore more than anyone on this earth, and they hugged each other every night as John drifted off to dreamland. Good night, Archie. Say good night to John, Archie. Good night, John. Sleep tight, Archie. Love you, Archie. Sweet dreams. See you in the morning.

Archie did not tell him to clean his teeth or to brush his hair. Archie did not say 'Shoulders back, shoulder blades together, stand up straight'. Archie did not mind if it was a tennis ball or a cricket ball. Above all, he was steadfast in his belief that one day John would be a poet, a fine one, and a famous one. With their heads snuggled together on the pillow, Archie always listened to John's poems, even the first drafts, the second-rate rubbish and the third-rate flops. And, of course, he never went to the lavatory. Or wet the bed.

'Boy? Where are you, boy? I'm com-*ing*.'

Slipping deeper down under the blankets, and pulling Archie with him, John could hear his father's heavy footsteps coming up the stairs, he could see his egg-shaped head and his centre parting and his upright bearing and his black and white views, coming round the door into his bedroom and leaning over him, his bristly face scratching his skin, his arms like rods of iron, tugging Archie out of his grasp.

'What! What's this!'

The boy fought back, red in the face, wrenching.

'Time to stop this nonsense. You're a big boy now. This has got to end! Stop this! I said… *let… go!*'

John turned his head and bit him.

'You! Did you just bite me! You – !'

After his father had gone out his bedroom, sucking his wrist, staring at his wrist, banging into the door frame, cursing to himself, John waited a moment or two, then a moment or two more, then crept carefully downstairs, tiptoeing very quietly, and sat on the bend, lurking, as close as he dared to the bottom steps. His ears burning, he could hear his father roaring in the kitchen.

'Bessie. *Bess*-ie!'

'Yes, dear.'

'The boy.'

'Yes?'

'Not unwholesome, is he?'

'Oh, is he being silly? What's he up to now?'

'What's he up to! It's what he's not up to. He doesn't have any playmates.'

'I'm not so sure you're right there, Ernest. There's Wendy from down the road. I found him in the cupboard with her.'

'He doesn't climb trees. When he tries to kick a ball he hits it with his shin. As for climbing a rope or a wall bar, you can forget that.'

'He and Wendy were sitting side by side, holding hands.'

'He shows no interest in golf.'

'It was so sweet.'

'He can't catch. The last time I lobbed one gently at him it hit him smack on the nose.'

'He's on the delicate side, dear. And you're bullying him a bit.'

'Speak up, woman.'

'I said he's delicate.'

'Anaemic, you mean. I'll never be able to take him on the golf course. I'd die a thousand deaths.'

'Give him time, dear.'

'Time? How much time does he want? He's coming up thirteen.'

'Boys develop at different ages. He'll suddenly shoot up, you'll see.'

'Shoot? Don't talk to me about shooting. The last time he tried he couldn't find the safety catch. Nearly killed the lot of us.'

'He has other gifts.'

'A milksop for a son. With those teeth.'

He looked at the red marks on his wrist.

'He can't help his teeth, Ernest. None of us can help our teeth, dear. Mine ache all the time. And he loves reading and writing. You saw that poem of his, the one he showed to Mr T.S. Eliot.'

'Never heard of him.'

'Yes, you remember, the American master, you did see the poem. It was lovely. And it made me laugh.'

'Laugh? I can believe that. That I can believe because that's what he is, a laugh.'

'The school says he has quite a little gift. He'll surprise you, in the end.'

'It's all very well being a swot pot but it won't help him in the world, will it? Won't help him run the firm. He'll have to get on with the men... Let's hope this Marl-bor-ough place stiffens him up a bit. God knows it's costing enough.'

'Does he *have* to play that horrible rugger?'

'It's compulsory.'

'Oh, dear.'

'And I've got him the best boots money could buy. And there's one more thing, Bessie.'

'Yes, dear?'

He sucked his wrist.

'The teddy bear.'

'Archie, you mean?'

'Get rid of it.'

15 | A NICE LITTLE CHAT WITH BESSIE

He was lurking behind the sofa.
'Come round and sit down, John dear, and we can have a nice little chat amongst ourselves.'

His mouth was slightly open.

'As long as you don't wriggle.'

She tapped the seat next to her and he took a step forward, only to stop halfway.

'Your father is very busy today, John, so it's just the two of us, isn't that nice? He's on business. Tomorrow he's off shooting with his friends but it doesn't matter a bit to me that you don't like guns, John darling, because you're a very clever boy who's going to be a poet.'

John looked down and his thin fingers picked at a torn bit on the arm of a leather chair.

'Girls are nicer than boys, Mummy, aren't they?'

'Do you think so?'

'Yes.'

'Well, they're certainly different.'

'Are they?'

'Leave the chair alone, dear. Sit on it properly.'

'I wish I had some girls as friends.'

'Oh you will, you're such a handsome chap.'

'Can I have a motor bicycle when I grow up?'

Bessie smiled.

'We'll talk about that later but your father has had a word with me and between the two of us I've been thinking that we're going to make a nice comfy little bed for Archie in the top cupboard. I've found a secret little place for him, that's the best thing. Isn't that nice? So be a sweet boy, won't you, dear, and we'll pop up and do that because I love you more than anything and you'll always be English on your mother's side. Come and give your Mummy a big kiss.'

He stared at his feet and stood his ground.

'And you're not odd. You're not.'

She knew this because she had watched him pouring the tea.

16 | THE TANTALUS

How could he ever tell his father what it was like, really like, being a boarder at Marlborough, being away at school with nowhere to hide? That was not something any boarder could ever tell any father, least of all his, who had never been away to school himself.

You couldn't tell your father about *that*. Not when being beaten on your bare buttocks was costing your father so much money, particularly not when, one day, one day before too long, he would have to tell him about the firm.

★

When his father – as in the early days he liked to do – took young John to visit his factory at 36 Pentonville Road, N1, the boy's strong sense of smell often caused his gorge to rise. The nausea would start well before they arrived, beginning on the tram as he inhaled his father's second hand pipe smoke. Even when Ernest wasn't actually smoking it still came out of his heavy tweeds or his hat, or was it coming out of his pores and the hairs on his hands and the hairs in his nose and the hairs in his ears? His thick suits seemed to sweat pipe smoke, and by the end of the rumble and tumble tram journey the boy's skin usually felt clammy as he swallowed and swallowed and moved closer by the second to vomiting.

The effect of his father's strong tobacco was further compounded by his own apprehension, by the sense of dread at what he was going to encounter yet again inside those noisy sheds and huts and rooms – let alone the words he would read in the workmen's eyes. Those days, those factory visits, all rolled up into one dark cloud, one multi-layered miasmic smell.

As they stepped off the tram his father would stop him on the pavement and say,

'The more you listen the more you learn, and the more you learn the better.'

The boy stood there, trying not to be sick.

'You need a good grounding because one day it will all be yours.'

They moved along the pavement.

'Did you hear me?'

'Yes, father.'

'You're very quiet today, boy.'

'Am I?'

'And pale about the gills. What a pale clod of a thing you are altogether. No wonder you're no good at games. My only son and you can't play a thing. Who'd credit it?'

He was coming up fourteen – the Great War had recently

ended – and although bad blood was boiling under the surface this was in the days before his defiance became open. He did not yet dare tell his father that he did not want to go to Pentonville Road at all, and that there was little chance of him listening or learning from the workmen for the simple reason he had not the least intention of following his father into the family business, however lucrative. He detested the very thought of it.

How on earth could he tell anyone at school, at Marlborough of all places, that he was going into trade, into family trade? It must never come out. So much of his life must never come out. Never ever. Even thinking about it made him feel more sick because he had other more important things on his mind. For example, he had to remember to say *writing* paper not *note*-paper. For example, he had to remember to pronounce envelopes (be they brown or white) as *on*-velopes not *en*-velopes. Never ever *en*-velopes.

But for now, on these journeys, he would keep his eyes down. That was his best option. He pretended that this visit to Pentonville Road was not happening and as a rule he was quite good at pretending that things were not happening or at pretending that things that were not happening were happening. When all was said and done he was a writer.

To divert himself and to stop dry-retching, he tried to come up with some rhymes, as many of his best poems had been written on trains or trams, on the move, poems going somewhere or impatient to be going somewhere, or anywhere. But on the way to Pentonville Road no rhymes would ever come.

The Works may have been only a few miles on the trams across London but it could as well have been a thousand. The smells would hit the boy the moment the front door of the factory opened, smells so different and so alien to him, so different from church and hassocks and cassocks.

'Ring the bell, boy.'

He kept his eyes down, down on the pavement.

'Can I have my ginger beer soon?'

'Go on, ring it! '

He took out his handkerchief and blew his nose as loudly as he could. His father hated the way his son blew his nose.

'*Ring it!*'

He rang the bell and on the instant the front door snapped wide open and a spruce man stood there like a jack-in-the-box. Mr Ernest was here. The Master and his son, Betjemann and Son, were visiting. They were expected. Look sharp there!

'This is my son. This is the boy. Yes, a fourth generation Betjemann, the next in line.'

Oh no, he wasn't.

I am not a chip off the old block.

You may belong here, father, but I do not.

Once inside, the spruce jack-in-the-box slid away, and his father left him for The Counting House. Left alone he was allowed – no, if left alone Master John was *expected* – to wander freely from room to room, from shed to hut. It was a little royal tour. As well as listening and learning and mugging the ways of the factory up like a swot pot, he was also, like a Field Marshal, meant to be *inspecting*.

One door led to another, one shed to another shed, with expert craftsmen, heads lowered, busying themselves in each place. He poked his young head and protruding teeth round door after door, room after room. There were the cabinet makers with their planes and their lathes, the silversmiths, the locksmiths, the engravers, the French polishers, the packers, the stock rooms, the timber yard, the patent office, the show rooms, and the yellow-faced clerks with their pencils stuck behind their ears. And he could not avoid seeing or hearing his name everywhere:

Betjemann

The Betjemann boy

The boy Betjemann

Betjemann's (founded 1820)

Betjemann's a German spy

The eyes of the workmen stole glances at him. Three or four of them, mostly the older ones who accepted rank and understood station, spoke deferentially to him:

'You the Master's son?'

'Yes, I am.'

'Master John, isn't it?'

'Yes, it is.'

Some, mostly the young apprentices, were surly and resentful. Or were they simply wary? One or two offered to show John what part they played in making the dressing tables or the mahogany cocktail cabinets or the onyx cigarette boxes or, the firm's pride and joy, the famous Betjemann tantaluses, but he could never hold their eyes or find anything to say, so, gawping and sniffing, he shuffled aimlessly from place to place.

What did he smell?...

Gas and oil, polish and veneer and sawdust and sweat, scalding metal and whining saws and singed leather, all combining in a heady, heavy mix. It clung to his skin and it stuck in his throat. To kill time rather than to see what else he could learn, he climbed ladders or escaped up the dusty back stairs.

'Be careful, Master John. Steep up there.'

Also, and pressingly, he wanted a pee but how on earth – who on earth – could he ask? So, while the king was in his counting house balancing the books and checking the ledgers weren't smudged, his son and heir was sniffing his way round the factory and crossing his legs until he found a tin bucket in a dark corner and rushed it too much and tucked it away too soon and left his pants a little wet.

Later, with the front door soon snapping shut behind them,

they were ushered out on the street and on to the slippery cobbles and on their way back home, a combative father and a surly son, side by side in the tram.

His father was once more sitting in his cloud of pipe smoke. John looked out of the window, with the London rain now sheeting down, and counted all the churches they passed, hassocks and cassocks, Church of England, Roman Catholic, Methodist, Baptist, rich man, poor man, beggar-man, thief, and willed the silence that sat between them to lengthen.

It had to come to a head.

His father was seething. He jingled his change in his pocket. John felt a quiver of sympathy for him, just a quiver, but his lips stuck to his teeth and his heart steeled. After a while, with his patience sorely tried, his father started to speak in loud, clipped syllables:

'So, what did you make of it?'

'I'm afraid I —'

'Don't mumble at me.'

'I wasn't — '

'I asked what did you make of it?'

'Nothing much, Father.'

'Nothing much? I think you can do better than that!'

He spoke so forcefully the passengers in front turned round, but he could not help himself.

'For heaven's sake, what were you up to, what were you doing with yourself as you went round? Did you not think to ask the men some questions? Yes? No? I thought we agreed that you would at least do *that*, I thought we agreed that at least you would *try* to learn. Come on, give me your sixpenny worth.'

Sing a song of sixpence.

The king was in his counting house,
Counting out his money.

The queen was in the parlour,
Eating bread and honey.

'Not a word for the cat! They may not be poets, John, but they're all artists, they're all craftsmen to their fingertips, their work is sought after in Harrods and in Asprey's, and God help me they'll all look up to you. That's their way. You think you're a cut above them, don't you? Think yourself a poet, don't you! You're so par-*tic*-u-lar. And maybe your mother and I have encouraged that by sending you away to school. Your education has got between us. You and your books have broken up the family. I saw that in there just now, saw it clear as day. My men are good men and good workers but you think they're too humble for you.'

In his disobliging silence the boy stared out of the window.

'They never have a free moment from dawn to dusk and what they do every day of the week for me in there pays the bills. To pay for *what*?'

Bad blood was now boiling all over the tram.

'To pay for your education, you droopy little prude. To pay for my milksop of a son. But, oh no, he's far too grand, isn't he! Far too grand to speak to the men who fix the engines or make the chairs he sits on. I'll tell you what you are, and I'll tell you once and for all.'

The boy spoke loudly back, but without looking into his father's grey, wounded eyes.

'What am I, Father?'

'You're not a fourth generation Betjemann at all, no, you're a slur on my name and you… you can go hang.'

And the boy's ears burnt but he went on looking out of the tram window, and the chanting rhythm resumed and the words went round and round in his head,

The maid was in the garden,
Hanging out the clothes,

When down came a naughty boy
And pecked off her nose.

17 | A BASKET CASE, 1921

The older John Betjeman had told the story so often, polished it so well, edited it so skilfully, he was not even sure if it was true, or how true it was. The first sentence that came back was…

'I'll see you tonight, Betjemann.'

And he was back there, back at Marlborough in the early 1920s, a boy again.

The second sentence was:

'They're going to put you in the basket tonight, yes, *you*, Betjemann.'

Said to him when he was thirteen or fourteen, those were, and indeed always would be, the two most terrifying sentences he ever heard: two sentences to a slow and lingering death. The first, 'I'll see you tonight, Betjemann' was the line used by any prefect who had decided for some reason that he was going to beat you. 'Tonight' was after prep and prayers but before you went up to bed in your dormitory. 'Tonight' was 9.15 sharp in the upper bathroom.

And the prefect had decided to beat you because? Well, for anything really. Because you were involved in a pillow fight or mobbing or had been throwing bread or had been spotted walking on a certain patch of grass or were (in Betjemann's case) incorrectly dressed or had (in Betjemann's case) been impertinent or 'lippy'. Or you could, of course, have broken any one of a hundred little school rules to do with ties or shoes or how many of your waistcoat buttons were to be done up or you had trespassed into places forbidden to someone in your lowly year. Being lippy or being above yourself in a wide range of ways was *asking for it*.

Oh yes, it all came flooding back.

Once you had been told 'I'll see you tonight, Betjemann' you had to endure all the lessons, get through lunch (no appetite), games (no talent), play rehearsals (oh, temporary bliss), late afternoon school, tea (no appetite, dry mouth), not long now, prep and prayers. With your fate drawing nearer minute by minute, the day seemed to stretch out for a week, with this long black cloud blocking out the sun and with the school's old waste pipes seeming to chuckle.

In an attempt to divert his anxiety he would think of Cornwall. Yes, good plan, think of Cornwall. In the early years, before they got a place of their own, they had stayed in a guest house at the bottom of Daymer Lane, oh, what was it called? Come on. Yes! It was called The Haven, and it was a haven.

Then (to stop thinking of the beating ahead) he forced himself to set off on an imaginary walk from The Haven round the springy turf of the headland, when

> *roller into roller curled*
> *And thundered down the rocky bay,*
> *And we were in a water-world*
> *Of rain and blizzard, sea and spray,*
> *And one against the other hurled*
> *We struggled round to Greenaway.*

And on along the headland towards Polzeath, with the sea a waterfall of whiteness on his left, and then, past Polzeath, keep it going, keep it going, there was the long steepish pull up to Pentire Point and the Rumps and on to Port Quin and Port Isaac. Port Isaac was a fair hike.

But calling to mind such memories brought only the briefest of respites. So, when this tactic started to run out on him, he would recite poems, incantatory ones that could induce a semi-catatonic state, such as *Do you remember an inn, Miranda, do you remember an inn*, no it can't have been that, can it, that poem was not written until later, it was *I remember, I remember, the house where I was born, the little window where the sun came peeping in at morn*, or he would hum to himself *I dream of Jeanie with the light brown hair*, the lovely Jeanie he once carried on the handlebars of his bicycle all the way to Blisland Church on the edge of Bodmin Moor.

Think of girls.

Yes, girls. That might help. What was it like being a girl? It was quite a thought and he thought about it quite a lot. He had spent hours being a girl on stage and he found he gloried in it, with his heart hammering in the wings before he came on, with his mother proudly watching and his deaf father dying a thousand deaths.

Whatever his parents were feeling in their wooden seats in the audience, he would rather be fitting on falsies and mincing across the stage than working in Pentonville Road, anything was better than being in his father's factory. He loved using a girl's voice and adopting a girl's gait and wearing make-up and having a big beauty spot on his cheek (as sported by Lady Teazle).

Acting in general and being a girl in particular afforded him a foot in both worlds, and it allowed him a chance to play bo-peep with his father, to send a message, to get away with things in his undercover way and to fall into himself and, best of all, to feel alive as he never had before.

The next year he was Maria in *Twelfth Night* and he loved being her as much as he loved being Lady Teazle in *School for Scandal*: he was a serving wench (Maria) *and* he was a snob (Lady Teazle), playing both ends of the social scale, and the irony of being cast in those roles was not entirely lost on him, as at school he sensed (but did not admit) that he was little more than a serving wench to the upper classes while in the holidays he was little more than a little snob with his parents.

The girls' parts were, of course, all taken by boys. Boys were all there were. Well, there was Matron, and there was the odd housemaster's wife popping up in chapel, but no what you might call gels, no one you allowed your mind to wander over. You spent all your days in all boys classrooms being taught by men, all your afternoons on games fields being tackled by boys and refereed by men with nobbly knees, and all your nights, lights out, say no more, in all boys dormitories.

Even being a girl on stage did not entirely liberate him or lift his miserable spirits for long. Try though he might to blank out the punishment that awaited him in the upper bathroom at 9.15 at night, there was no inoculation against reality. Any hopes of a decent day were dashed on the rocks by those prefectorial sentences, *I'll see you tonight, Betjemann*, any hopes were wrecked on that Doom Bar in Wiltshire, and every stretched-out minute led to the moment when, at 9.15 sharp, he went in his pyjamas to bend down in the bathroom (with his head under the sink) to take whatever was coming. Being able to *take it* was crucial, he was told, particularly if, like Betjemann, you had *asked for it*.

Prefects beat your bottom with the heel of a leather slipper or with the heel of a whippy plimsoll. Only a master could use a cane. The cane was worse. Prefects were limited to giving you four whacks with a slipper. Masters, if they felt it appropriate, and they often felt it was, could go up to six strokes. The heel of a leather slipper left a red half moon mark on your presented bum, whereas the cane left railway track ridges of blue and purple and yellow. You had to bend right over and position yourself in that way under the sink so that if you were unable to take it, if you were a coward who came up too quickly in the middle of the beating, you cracked the back of your head, a condign punishment.

So he did his prep – his Latin and Greek and History, his Caesar and Xenophon and the Tudors and Stuarts – with a dry mouth and a sinking gut. Each time, before setting off to the bathroom, he prayed, hands together eyes closed, knowing that in all likelihood the Almighty would be inexplicably indifferent but he was still going to give himself one last chance, give Him one last chance, lodging one last appeal, mumbling and tumbling out his desperate words:

'Dear God,

Please protect me. Please make it not hurt too much. I mean I know it will hurt, of course it will, if you thrash a bony bum like mine it is going to hurt, but make it not hurt *too* much please. I was cheeky, it's true, I can't deny it. I did tell Philpott he was a prick. He claims I called him a big prick and I want to make it absolutely clear that I did not. I called him a little prick. My exact words were, "You're a little prick, Potty, with a beta minus brain." Because he is. And his eyes leapt out of their sockets. He went off the handle.

I'm trying to be good, God, I really am, but it doesn't seem to be working as I tend to find it fun to go one more than I need and I am finding that trying to be funny carries its own risks. In future I must try to be less funny, mustn't I?

Please, God, look after Mother and Father. I often don't behave as a good son should with them. I do not honour them as a son should. And please look after Archie. I wish Archie was waiting for me in bed tonight because Archie always cheers me up. He always loves me and he never goes to the lavatory. But I daren't have him here in the dormitory with me. It's unimaginable, having him in bed with me in dorm, it's unthinkable. If I did bring him back to school they would never lay off.

I've been called a miserable misfit a few times and I'll settle for that because one day I will go to Oxford and be a poet and be a triumphant misfit. But it looks as if it's all going to take a bit longer than I thought. I'm so unhappy I'm numb and I would like to die. Truly I would. I tried to write a poem about it all, about waiting for the coffin lid to be nailed down, but it wouldn't come, there was no muse in sight. Please look after Mother and Father. No, I've said that already. I don't want them to be any angrier with me than they are. Please make me good, or at least please make me better.'

But 'I'll see you tonight, Betjemann' was small beer, it was as nothing next to sentence two, often said by a boy out of the corner of his mouth while passing you in the corridor, 'They're going to put you in the basket tonight, Betjemann.'

The scene, he remembered only too well, was always set in the same place: in a big room called Big School, a huge bare space in the middle of the school's oldest buildings, the room where the teaching used to take place in the days or the centuries before individual classrooms were built.

In winter there was an open fire at both ends of Big School. At one end was Big Fire where the bloods and prefects lounged with their acolytes. Around Big Fire there was always plenty of room for the select few. At the far end of the room, at the lower end of the social scale, was Little Fire. Here large numbers of boys gathered like a crowd before a house match final, an unruly and jostling mob trying to warm their chilblained hands. To feel any warmth coming through the rough and tumble of Little Fire you needed to be armed with broad shoulders and sharp elbows. Betjemann only had a sharp tongue.

There were two huge waste paper baskets into which the most skilful cricketers would throw, with deadly accuracy, apple cores and tightly screwed up balls of inky paper. It was as if they were throwing into the wicketkeeper's gloves. He himself could not throw for toffee. Not only did Betjemann play girls on stage, he threw like one.

No one knew how or why anyone was picked on to be basketed. It was baffling. Oh, the mystery of schoolboy power!

Oh, the inscrutable subtlety of bullying! One morning you could somehow sense your fate from the particular way you were being looked at or the particular way you were being ignored. Your nostrils twitched at some new smell in the haunted air, or your ears picked up a barely heard whisper, and you knew your number was up. Or you saw someone else, another poor sod, being pointed at or pointedly ignored and your heart leapt buttercup high, it wasn't you after all, you'd got away with it, and a small skiff of hope pushed off from the shore.

But no.

Suddenly a group of four or five senior boys would stand up and come over and surround you, grab your arms and legs, pinion you, take your clothes off, pour red paint over you and put you in the basket. The basket would then be hauled slowly up on a thick rope, creaking and groaning with the extra weight, to about head height where you were left swinging while the other boys came and looked through the slats at you or dropped things on your head. It was a hushed ritual in a zoo, with breath held quiet.

Ten minutes or so before prep was due to begin the basket was lowered in jerks, creaking and groaning to the floor, where, your teeth chattering with the cold, you were handed back your clothes. As you pulled on your trousers and hurried out with as much dignity as you could muster, everyone in Big School stamped so hard it seemed to shake the foundations of the building.

You ran to the bathroom in your boarding house and scrubbed the paint off as best you could, not easy with your hands trembling, more a smearing than a cleansing, and then you grabbed your books and ran back across the quad to the prep room, doing up your tie as you ran, before explaining in breathless bursts to the master who was taking prep why you were late.

The room was electric and taut as you entered. If you dared to lean forward and say, as quietly as you could, 'The thing is, sir… I've been basketed,' the master would only look blankly back as if you were speaking in Old Norse or Faroese. So you said nothing. The master looked up, nodded and said 'Sit down, Betjemann,' and waved you to your seat and impassively returned to his pile of marking.

18 | BACK IN THE CLASSROOM, 1928

At this preparatory school in Cockfosters, reached by way of the Piccadilly Line, he was back once again to the smell of stale biscuits and warm plimsolls and has anyone seen my pencil case. But, this time, with a difference. A big difference. At twenty- two he was now *Mr.* Betjeman, a teacher or (if you prefer the classier term) a schoolmaster, but beyond question a grown-up, if not an adult who was more than ready to be called sir, and trying his very best to look the part, but fearful that the eagle-eyed boys would soon enough rumble him, spotting that he wore no academic hood in chapel, and preparing to pounce as a pack on this visible sign of no degree.

He had, however, decided to start his teaching career with a bit of a bang. In cricketing terms, not that he saw life in cricketing terms, he would attack the bowling, he would immediately get on to the front foot, move towards the ball and smack, if not smite, it to all parts. With this purpose, he strode down the corridor, like Moses cutting a path, like Moses parting the waves of small boys, and he felt better and stronger for the striding, for the parting, indeed steelier by the second, and once over the threshold of his classroom he slammed the door as hard as he could behind him.

'Right, sit down please. There's absolutely no need to stand up for me, not that all of you were.'

On he strode across the room and up he stepped, with a hard step, bang, on to the dais.

'And get some paper out, we're having a quick test. What? No, I haven't got any paper, you're meant to bring your own, we're to encourage you at all times to be responsible for your own lives. When he appointed me, the headmaster was very clear indeed on that, as I find Mr Hope is on most things. By the way, what a good name that is for a headmaster – Mr Hope – don't you think, and definitely better than Mr Despair.'

He paused – a longish pause, if a little on the hammy side – but the boys, he was pleased to see, were already glancing sideways at each other, thinking what on earth was he going on about now. Perfect, just the job, exactly the response he wanted, so on he went:

'Which reminds me, there was a headmaster of another school, a school where dim cousins used to go, a school not a million miles from here where there was a headmaster who went by the name of Cope, and all the boys used to call him Can't, which I think is jolly cruel, but then I know only too well that boys like you can be cruel and, sadly enough, or funnily enough, some cruel things do make one laugh. And laughter can bring us all closer together, don't you agree?'

One or two of the class smiled a little nervously at him as if he were a dog who had got loose and might easily turn nasty. At which he started to walk back and forth across the dais, a strut he had rehearsed the evening before in his bedroom, three steps to the right, swivel on his heel, turn, three steps to the left, swivel on his heel, turn. Then, to keep them on the edge of their seats, he suddenly stepped down on to the wooden floor and moved smartly through the tightly packed rows of ink-stained desks, flapping the wide sleeves of his gown like a pantomime crow. On the wall at the back of the classroom hung a large and faded map of The Ancient World.

'Right,' he said, 'pens ready, we are kicking off with a twenty questions test, if my imagination runs to twenty, and I will begin with a very easy one.'

He was, he realised, already sounding like some of his old Marlborough masters, echoing their phrases, reprising their catch-words, and he found the parody rather fun.

'Ready? Come along, come *along*! Make haste. Question one, what is the worst school in England?'

He glared challengingly round the classroom.

'I'll repeat the question because I can see that some of you infant prodigies *still* haven't got your pens ready. Question one, what is the worst school in England? Eyes front, everyone, no cheating. Time's up. Yes, you're correct, the answer is Marlborough College, no quibbling, my decision is final. Marlborough it is, by clear blue water. You can all now put that down. So, congratters everyone, you've all got two marks. Ex-cell-ent.'

The boys grinned and nodded and wrote many and various mis-spellings of Marlborough. Having done that, they put a big tick next to their answers, and awarded themselves the two marks on offer. They had to admit that so far Bengerman, if a bit rabid, didn't seem such a bad bloke.

'And there's no need,' he said, 'to swap papers. Mark your own. That's how trusting a teacher I am, because trust is such an important thing in life, don't you agree, and I do trust you, well, after a quick check of your faces, most of you. Maybe that is unwise of me, but on balance I would rather be a trusting person and found to be wrong in some of my judgements than a hard-bitten cynic who prides himself on the fact that he is never fooled.'

The boys looked blank. One boy shouted out,

'Why Marlborough College, sir?'

'I've often wondered myself.'

'No, why is Marlborough College the correct answer, sir?'

'Because I was a boy there for five years from 1920 to 1925, so I should know.'

'But that's where I'm going.'

'Bad luck, chum. And to think that my parents, Mr and Mrs Betjemann, to think that Ernest and Bess Betjemann, yes, for those are their Christian names, to think that by sending me to Marlborough College my parents believed that I would be going up in the world. They believed that at Marlborough College I would come into my own, that at Marlborough College I would become presentable and get on, and that one day perhaps my fame would travel even further abroad.'

'Are you famous already, then, sir?'

'Not yet, give me a chance. Anyway, they thought that their only child, their rather common little boy, would learn at Marlborough not to heap food on his plate, would learn to speak nicely and to stand up for himself, would learn to get round people, never to be a sneak, and, more importantly, they hoped that he would develop some social ease and so move up the social scale, rather than be stuck where we were, halfway up and halfway down, like Humpty Dumpty, when all I wanted was not to be bullied and to be left alone to grow my hair long and be a poet.'

'Is that why your hair is long, sir?'

'Well, obviously.'

'Mr Hope hasn't any hair, sir.'

'Exactly. But remind me later to tell you a bit more about my parents, to whom I was – and indeed still am – a great disappointment, and then you can tell me all about yours.'

Come to think of it, he could tell them so many stories about his own life, for example the one when he was a basket case at Marlborough or the one when he visited his father's factory. This teaching lark was easy: a captive audience and a chance to tell them any old story you liked, sure in the knowledge it would come up as fresh as a daisy.

'And it's just occurred to me, oh what an ex-cell-ent idea, for prep tonight I want you to write me a composition or – if you want a simpler word – a *piece* entitled "My father and my mother", and I will take those in on Monday. Hang on, do you have me on Mondays?'

'Yes, sir,' they chorused.

'Yes, you lucky boys, you do, and on Monday we can all compare notes. It'll be as much fun as going to confession. Write as much as you like or as little as you like, but be sure to give me the gossip. I don't want flawless fair copies I want the low-down, and the lower down the better. Fathers and sons... I mean, *what* a topic! And whatever you come up with, whatever you say on fathers and sons or mothers and sons, I won't split on you, promise.'

He raised his arms like a conductor before the first note, like a large crow before take-off.

'Listen! You may write in prose or in poetry, it's up to you. Prose will do perfectly well but poetry is the shorthand of the heart, but in whichever *genre* you choose to write about your parents, do try to entertain me.'

'Mr. Benchman?'

'Yes, more or less.'

'What does *genre* mean?'

'It means kind of writing, category, overall style. Don't they teach you anything in French?'

'No, sir. Nothing,' the class cried.

'Sir?'

'Yes.'

'About our prep.'

'Yes yes, what about it?'

'What if you haven't got any parents?'

'Oh, I'm so sorry, I hadn't thought of that.'

'That's all right, sir.'

'How insensitive of me. I feel absolutely routed. Dear boy,

don't you remember them at all?'

'No, I've got some, sir, but Massingham-Fowler hasn't.'

'Massingham-Fowler? Which one of you is Massingham-Fowler? Is Massingham-Fowler here?'

'No, sir, he's in Mr Pandy's class.'

'So he is not relevant.'

'Shall I tell him that, sir?'

'Do. And it's charming of you to take so much trouble.'

He stepped briskly back up on to the dais, or (better word) on to the rostrum, in a look-at-me way, as if he were lord of the manor and monarch of all he surveyed, and with a sweep of his eyes looked down on the class, or as he preferred to think of them, on his boys, or (as he sometimes pronounced the word) his *byes*.

'Now, *byes*, for a few bits of advice on writing. Pens out. Make haste. Pens out!'

He waited for the rustling and the scuffling to settle. He waited for their attention, with a hint of threat, and then launched himself:

'When you write, do say what you think, but remember that if you want to say something profound you are better advised to be plain and simple in your expression. That's the trick. That's how we avoid a collision of clichés. Poetry is not a crossword puzzle. When we write from the heart, *byes*, we write best. Look in thy heart, Sir Philip Sidney said, and write. And old Sir Philip knew a thing or two about writing, I can tell you. Being plain and simple hits hard. Being plain and simple hits home, because it's the heat and the emotion under the simple words that counts. Someone else said that before me, I cribbed that, can't remember from whom, an American, come to me in a minute. Oh, who cares.'

A boy put his hand up.

'Mr Benjamin?'

'Not a bad shot, but yes.'

'Could you give us some examples?'

'Examples?'

'Yes, please, sir,' the class shouted in overlapping waves. He raised a palm to stem the tide.

'But *should* I be giving you examples? Isn't that tantamount to doing your wretched prep for you?'

'Oh, go on, sir.'

'Oh, all right, I will.'

He sat on the edge of a front row desk, and went on in gentler tones:

'For example, "I hate my father". That is a good sentence.'

'Do you hate your father, sir?'

He slammed his palm on a desk.

'What did you just say?'

'I asked if you hated your father, sir? Because I love my father.'

'I missed your name. Do you have a calling card?'

'It's Stevenson.'

'Well, Stevenson, we are talking about writing, we are talking about sentences, not people. *Sentences.* Here's another one. "My father took me on long, silent walks." That isn't a bad sentence. "My mother battles with her weight". Not bad either. "My mother bores me." Now, that is a good sentence. In other words, fire the ammunition with a light touch. Write simple English, but push the boundaries of the sayable. And the last thing, because I can hear you shuffling your feet and see you chewing your pens, and I know you would much rather get back to carving your names on the desks, the last bit of advice I have to offer is that you read what you have written out loud to yourself and see how it sounds. That will help you develop an ear for your sentences. A good sentence has a musical feel, and you should listen for that sound, for that music. If your writing sounds like you at your musical best it's probably jolly good.'

Feeling he had given rather good advice, if not too good, if not casting phoney pearls before some real swine, he walked to the open classroom window and looked out over the playing fields to the cricket pavilion and beyond. Smelling the grass, he sneezed (as he often did in the summer) once, twice, bless you, John, as Mumsie used to say, sneeze, sneeze, three times, four times, bless you. He took his large red and white spotted handkerchief out of the sleeve of his jacket, where he liked it to dangle on display, and blew his nose with a flourish, before continuing to speak with his back turned to the class.

'Gosh, look at the mower chugging away on the cricket pitch.'

He heard two or three boys stand up in a clatter and rush to join him at the window.

'No, sit down! Stop shoving! I did not mean get out of your desks and physically look at it, I meant *consider* the view. How literal-minded you are. Shoo!'

They resumed their seats and he resumed his performance.

'I bet the groundsman is enjoying his work on the pitch this morning. What a happy, healthy life a school groundsman must lead! Like a man in a Cowper poem. No, more a Goldsmith. How I envy him, a son of the soil, all that grass and fresh air and the sun shining on his nutmeg head. Just surveying the scene before me brings back *The Deserted Village*, the pastoral poem by Oliver Goldsmith, which my father often read to me, this was in the days when we were getting on and we were holidaying on the Norfolk Broads. And, by the way, you'll notice as you get to know me better that I slip into poetry from time to time, because I am a poet, so make sure you listen out for my rhymes getting rummer and rummer.'

'I hate poetry,' a boy shouted from the back row.

'Ah, not only a dim little cousin but a smug little Philistine. And before you ask what a Philistine is, you may find out more if you read your Bible, in this instance the Books of Joshua and

Samuel. And I hate to say this during your chicken-pox, Pitts-Higgins, and do keep taking the potions, but you're being jolly rude.'

'Sor-*ry*.'

'Bit missing?'

'Sor-*ry*, *sir*.'

'Better. Anyway, I was talking of my father. On one particular occasion – I remember it as if it were yesterday – he read Goldsmith out loud to me when we were moored at Coltishall, and by out loud I mean very out loud because he was and is as deaf as a post. I have a father who knows the name of every bird in the British Isles but hears no birdsong. Hang on. Have I got that bit wrong?'

'What bit, sir?'

'Birdsong, sir?'

'No no, I called it the cricket *pitch*. Shouldn't I have called it the *wicket*? Or is it the *square*?'

'You should know, sir.'

'Should I?'

'You are the master in charge of cricket, sir.'

He swivelled round and took a deep bow.

'Oh, my goodness me, so I am. Good point. But no more red herrings, back to the test, because we're up and off in the novices handicap hurdles and at the moment we're all level pegging, all neck and neck in first place on two marks each, and it's terribly exciting and here comes question number two.'

They picked up their pens.

'Question number two is, what is Matron's nickname, and, no, I will not accept Old Crackpot.'

'I like Matron, sir.'

'You do, do you, jolly good, and I have absolutely no wish to come between the two of you. Moving on, question three, moving on, question three, you'll notice I am repeating myself to allow the stragglers amongst you to catch up, that's what teachers do, that's what teachers do, and question three is who is T.S. Eliot? Write down all you know about T.S. Eliot. You have two minutes for this. But before you do so, boys, what do you think of Miss Hoskins, the games mistress?'

'What do *you* think, sir?'

'Why not ask her out, sir?'

'Why not give her one... of your poems, sir?'

'Oh, what a good idea! Why don't I address her in verse?'

'What would you say, sir?'

'D'you know I'm not sure, but give me a minute. Well, orf the top of my head I'd probably say something along the lines of:

Were you a prefect and head of your dormit'ry?
Were you a hockey girl, tennis or gym?
Who was your favourite? Who had a crush on you?
Which were the baths where they taught you to swim?

I say, boys, what a stroke of luck! Miss Hoskins, like a vision, appears. She's going across the quad at this very moment. Just look. Now, that's my kind of gel. She's a bit of all right, isn't she? Not Miss Lob the Lesbian but a sort of Bonzo Trouncer, an Aphrodite in shorts, a tigress of the tennis courts, windblown and sporty. Just imagine... those suntanned forearms whizzing them over the net. Those thighs! Wouldn't you like to be the saddle on *her* bike?'

19 | LUNCH ON TOP TABLE, 1928

It was a red letter day when Mr Hope asked Mr Betjeman to join him for lunch. Lunch at top table was a call from on high, a treat not available to all, a privilege indeed to be seated right beneath the honour boards and the founder's portrait. The music master, for example, had never been invited to enjoy his lunch in this influential company, not once, a grievance and a grudge that made him more likely than ever to deafen the congregation during the organ voluntary.

If you were not invited to the top table, assistant masters were required to do their duty. Doing your duty meant you had to sit at the end of a longer and noisier table of boys and to dish out the mince and the spotted dick or the cauliflower cheese and the jam roly-poly. The assistant master would find a stack of plates piled high in front of his place, and once he had carefully divided up and served the food, he and the boys on either side of him were expected to keep a civilised conversation going, though this mutually spasmodic effort was mostly drowned out by an onslaught of scooping and scraping. Facing the assistant master at the far end of each boys' table would be the supposedly moderating influence of a female. Matron and Mrs Hope and (more obviously) Miss Hoskins were female.

On this occasion, the selection for top table could not have worked out better for Mr Betjeman because Miss Hoskins had also been invited to join the circle, and was hurrying hot-footed from the gym, down dark corridors and past rows of hooks and lockers and through heavy doors, rushing into the dining room a little late, a little flushed and, most of all, in her shorts.

Not long after grace, while those on top table were being slowly served by elderly kitchen staff, Mr Hope leant forward to speak to Mr Betjeman. But first, before we hear that conversation, a word or two about Mr Hope. He was one of those Old Etonian communists who liked to beat a boy with a number four cricket bat, a man who enjoyed nothing more than to walk around the grounds, to inspect the cricket square, have a word with the under gardener and return to find the butler hard at work cleaning the family silver.

Recent years had also, he felt, provided proof for his happy prediction on the future of the world; recent history allowed Mr Hope to sing the praises of Stalin and his modernisation and five-year plans. Mr Hope had five-year plans of his own, though he was undecided on whether the long-haired Mr Betjeman would be a part of them.

'How are things, Mr Betjeman?'

'Very well, Headmaster.'

'English going well?'

'I think so, Headmaster.'

'You *think* so? That doesn't sound very good. You've got to lead the boys, to keep the game moving forward, to keep up their energy and their spirits. Cricket going well?'

'Very well indeed.'

'Good, good. Tell them to pitch the ball up. Pitch it UP.'

Here he banged the table, a loud noise which made the assistant cook – who was passing by with a tray of large water jugs – jump and nearly lose control of the lot.

'Putting it another way,' the headmaster went on, 'don't bowl short.'

'That is exactly what I tell them, Headmaster.'

'Forward and back defensives coming along?'

'Very nicely, Headmaster.'

'Good man. How's young Stevenson doing?'

'Oh very well.'

'Good family. His father could play a bit. Played for the Gentlemen of Hertfordshire. Opening batter.'

'Gosh.'

'Any good keepers?'

Completely lost now, Mr Betjeman thought it best not to have heard that one.

'Schools could learn a lot, you know, Betjeman, from the way things are going in Russia. None of this wishy-washy nonsense. Stalin would lead a good school, I've often thought that. The man's got a steady eye. I'd appoint him like a shot. He would sort the boys out, pick the right team, draw up lists, give clear orders, and see them carried out to the letter. No qualms about it. You may not know this, Betjeman, but that's what his name means, Stalin means a man of steel, a man with grip. He has a firm handshake, a hand that grips, and he sees clearly that inefficiency is the blight. Yes, we could learn a lot from him.'

'Oh, I'm sure.'

'Meant to ask you, Betjeman.'

'Yes, Headmaster?'

'Are you thinking of schoolmastering as a career?'

'I'm certainly enjoying it so far.'

'But you're not one of those here-today-gone-tomorrow fellows, are you? You know what sticking means? You understand the spirit of a school? Good, good. Each of us must do his bit. Each man must be responsible and reliable. We'll review things later when you've got a few more weeks under your belt. Any schoolmasters in your family?'

'No, Headmaster, none at all. They went their different ways.'

'What sort of ways? The Church? The law? What does your father do?'

'He's a manufacturer. He makes cabinets and all manner of luxury goods.'

'Does he, by Jove.'

Mr Hope, bemused by the phrase 'luxury goods', pointed to Mr Betjeman's plate.

'Do start. After all that teaching you'll be in need of sustenance.'

'Thank you. As a matter of fact my father designed the first tantalus.'

'What? The tantalus? The contraption you lock the decanters in, the thingy that keeps your servants from stealing your drink?'

'Yes, it's his invention. I think I may have seen one on your sideboard. The triple decanter with the mahogany finish?'

'Saves me a fortune. Marvellous, must be a clever chap, your father. First class idea.'

Betjeman decided to go for broke:

'And he's a big fan of Stalin. Father follows him to the letter in his factory.'

'So, no surprise he's doing well. The other thing... the other point I was going to make, was, I was walking past your classroom the other day and I couldn't help noticing.'

'Noticing what, Headmaster?'

'You trying to make yourself heard above the baying horde.'

'I think I'm right in saying, Headmaster, that what you may have been over-hearing was the crowd scene in *Julius Caesar*. Or one of the crowd scenes, I can't remember which, as there are quite a few in the play. You know the Roman mob, they don't listen, they shout first and then they run wild.'

'In which case it was a very convincing re-enactment.'

'I'm glad you thought so.'

'Wasn't ragging then?'

'No, and this whole class performance led on to their own original writing. We're all writing things, personal recollections, and sharing them. Reading them out loud.'

'Sounds on the risky side.'

Betjeman told himself he was saying far too much, altogether too much, but as was often the case he found himself unable to stem the tide.

'And I'm also writing a longer piece on boys and reading, boys and books. In fact, come to think of it, two of my Oxford friends were with me on the very day you mention, Mr Auden and Mr Waugh.'

'Over for a day's golf, were they?'

'No, joining in the lessons.'

'Schoolmasters, are they?'

'Writers.'

'But decent enough for all that?'

'Oh, they recited poems to the boys, and did some reading of their own work, nothing too decadent.'

Mr Hope, a head famously impervious to charm, did not take to young men who thought they were funny. It was said that telling a misjudged joke to Hope had done for many a beak. Sensing this, Mr Betjeman coughed nervously and hurried on:

'Joking aside, my friends loved everything about their visit.'

'Excellent. Our boys sense when not to let you down with outsiders. Good manners in the young, always a good thing.'

'And talking of plays, Headmaster.'

'Yes?'

Mr Hope's eyes were narrowing and wary.

'I was wondering if I could put one on next term.'

'A play?'

'Yes.'

'What sort of play?'

'A comedy I thought. The boys can be very funny.'

'Doesn't involve dressing up, does it?'

'Not too much. Hardly any.'

'Leads to poor behaviour, doesn't it, imitating members of staff, ways of speaking, ways of walking, that jeering kind of thing. I don't take to scoffing.'

'That certainly wouldn't happen, Headmaster, not with me at the helm.'

'The last play we had was closer to a shocker than a prank. I'll need to think about this one, Betjeman. Need to sleep on it.'

And with that, the headmaster turned his full attention to his food, releasing Mr Betjeman to talk to the person sitting on his right, Miss Hoskins, though it was she, having dabbed her full moist lips with her napkin, those lips shaped for sin, she who turned her blue eyes on him and spoke first,

'Why don't you come to the gym sometime, John?'

'The gym?'

'Yes, it's quite close to your classroom, but I don't think you've ever set foot inside.'

There were two shocks in her first sentence, two explosions, and they followed hard one upon the other, both in their different ways bringing an extreme reaction to his nervous system. One was the word *gym* and the other was the name *John*.

There was no three-letter word in the English language he hated or feared more than the word *gym*. Gym meant taking off your clothes. Gym meant revealing your legs. Gym meant springing and jumping and bouncing up and down. It was almost as bad as the phrase *well-built*. A gym was a prospect of future woe, a rallying point for bullies, a place for medicine balls and matting and racquets and parallel bars and vaulting horses and smelly socks, and worst of all a place where you strapped on boxing gloves and put up your guard and were hit and were supposed to shrug off little things like bruises and black eyes and nosebleeds.

The other shock was hearing Miss Hoskins speak his Christian name. John. *John*. She had never used it before and he had never heard a sound so sweet, so dancing with the daffodils. From *gym* to *John*, from three letters of prosaic hell to the heavenly poetry of four. Oh, Juliet, my throat is dry.

'Me, in the gym, yes, Miss Hoskins, why not?'

'Do come and I can show you the ropes.'

'Would you?'

'And we can climb the wall bars together, John, they're so good for co-ordination, and then we launch out side by side and swing down on the ropes.'

'That sounds wonderful fun.'

'It is. The boys love racing me right up to the top rung, the little devils. One or two are becoming quite forward.'

Was this the time to show some initiative in the face of forward boys, to come up with a firm counter invitation of his own, to strike while the iron was hot? Why not suggest that she might like to join him in visiting some local churches? There was one priceless architectural jewel close by, with a three-decker pulpit, and they could cycle out there together along the country roads. Or how about a day out at Oxford? He could show her everything, in Oxford there were no end of jewels on offer and he could be at his brilliant best. Or she could come to stay in Cornwall. How his parents would approve!

She was the cream in his coffee and he wanted to pour out his soul. With eyes aflame, he breathed her in and felt dizzy and nearly plunged at her over the jam roly-poly. But something about her forearms held him back. Why were all his girls big strong boys?

'Isn't this lunch good?' she said. 'I'm ravenous.'

20 | HETER OR HOMO?

How heter was he? How homo? How often he had asked himself this, wondering what percenter he was. Was he 80-20, or 50-50? It was difficult, wasn't it, to be completely sure if you were a bit queer, or fairly sure you were completely queer. And he realised that even raising the percentage question with some people brought the risk of you getting horsewhipped.

Even so, he had also often asked himself the tricky one, if heter equalled brawn, did homo equal brains? Did unhealthy homos, for example, read more books than hearty heters? Sometimes, judging by a puntful of Oxford homos, it seemed that it was so. And certainly some queers seemed much quicker at picking things up. So to speak.

But no, that must be nonsense. As was the talk of sensitive plants and knitted ties. Not all Philistines had muscles. Nor were all people with muscles Philistines. Perhaps, and this notion took his fancy, perhaps he was a girl in a boy's body. Perhaps it was nothing more than that: the physical and the mental sides in him were not quite evenly matched.

No, that wasn't right either.

He was a boy and he felt like a boy. He liked girls. He wanted to be with them. He had crushes on them all the time. When he closed his eyes and thought of being in bed with a girl, though, he had only the vaguest, blurriest picture of what happened next after you stopped kissing, unsure what there was still to do and exactly how it was to be done. Boys were easier. He could picture them all right. They were simpler. He'd seen hundreds of naked boys. He had also seen plenty of paintings of nude Cornish boys by Henry Scott Tuke. Besides, hadn't he been to a boarding boys' public school? That was powerful first hand experience. And wasn't he now teaching at a boarding boys' prep school?

But he had not seen a girl. Not properly. Not fully. Not yet.

It was a perfect day for cricket and, if it was possible to make a perfect day for cricket yet more perfect, Miss Hoskins did so by watching from the boundary edge, being right there as the drama in the middle unfolded. When she arrived, lying her bicycle on the recently mown grass, she waved to the new master-in-charge.

'Howzat?'

The long-haired umpire once again quickly raised his forefinger, saying,

'That is out.'

The batsman looked incredulous, shouting in a high treble back down the wicket:

'*Out?*'

'Yes, Stevenson, out.'

'How?'

'L.B.W. Or, if you don't know what that means, Leg Before Wicket.'

'But I *hit* it.'

'That's not my fault, Stevenson, off you go. Sorry about that, old chap. Time to allow some other young swashbuckler to come in and face the music.'

Stevenson stood his ground.

'If you hit the ball with your bat you can't be out L.B.W.'

'I'm not discussing the finer points with you, Stevenson.'

A few of the fielders started to rally round and to offer simultaneous advice to the aggrieved batsman:

'Lovely pads, Stevenson, just a pity they got in the way.'

'Off you go to the pavilion, pisspot.'

'Stevenson, you're a cretin.'

'You're crap, Stevenson, always have been, always will be. Crap.'

'*Byes, byes,*' said Mr Betjeman, 'there is absolutely no call for this abuse.'

'If you're given out, sir, you have to leave the field. You have to accept the umpire's decision. The umpire's decision is final.'

'It is one of the beauties of cricket, Mr Hope said. He spoke to us about that at assembly this morning, sir. You remember, sir.'

'He did indeed, good point, so off you jolly well go, Stevenson,' the cricket master said. 'Beat it, vamoose, scram!'

Stevenson crossed his arms.

'I'm not going because I wasn't out!'

Stevenson stood there glaring at Mr Betjeman and the cricket master, emboldened by the supporting cast of fielders, glared back at Stevenson:

'Don't you get uppity with me, young man. I've already had enough of you in class. And you are also out for arguing.'

The batsman's treble reached an even higher pitch:

'You can't be given out for that, I've read the laws, and what's more you don't even know how to give the batsman guard.'

'Yes, I do.'

'When I came in to bat you didn't even know what "middle and leg" meant.'

'And now you're also out for getting on my nerves and being a thumpingly disdainful bore. Forgive my candour, old stinker, but you're out on at least three accounts. And if you don't go you will be blown away in a deluge of impositions.'

'Right, that's it,' Stevenson screamed, unstrapping his pads and throwing one of them hard in the wicketkeeper's face. He then picked up his bat and started to windmill it above his head, whirling it faster and faster as he walked away from the crease towards the pavilion, before letting it go at full speed like a javelin, the bat narrowly missing the ducking Miss Hoskins who at that very moment was running on to the field, Oh, fair one! So adorably athletic! Running towards the umpire with the speed of a swallow and the grace of a boy.

Following her, to join in the fun, was Rufus, the grounds-man's ancient dog.

Miss Hoskins – his tennis-playing biking girl, his wholly to his liking girl – looked dazzling as she ran towards Mr Betjeman, all bouncing hair and soft curves and firm forearms, and with her big blue eyes wide open. As she reached the wicket, the whole fielding side came quickly round her in a very tight huddle.

'Mr.Betjeman,' she said, 'a word, if I may.'

'Yes, Miss Hoskins, of course.'

She turned her big blue eyes on the boys.

'In private. Boys! In Private!'

'Oooooooo.'

The cricket master stepped in.

'Stop that, *byes*. Move away, *byes*. Gentlemen, please.'

There was a distant sound of splintering damage in the pavilion.

'Further away, *byes*. Much further. *Shoo!*'

Miss Hoskins smiled and waited patiently for them to re-settle on another part of the field, a surly and restless pack. She was an absolute stunner. Oh, the tilt of her nose. He felt tipsy looking at her. Oh bliss. Oh love so pure it has to end! Then, she came even closer to him, and there was a tightening in his throat.

'The thing is, John, if you go on giving people out at this rate the game won't last very long.'

'But that's good, isn't it?'

'Is it? Why?'

'Mr Hope advised me to keep things moving, because then the boys don't get bored, he said, because bored boys can be dangerous boys. He did say that.'

'Did he?'

'He did. Clearly.'

'Well, there's keeping it moving and there's keeping it moving, and these boys are looking and sounding pretty dangerous to me already. You're already deep into the second innings and you've only been going twenty-five minutes.'

'Is that why there's rather a lot of swearing?'

'It could be.'

'I did wonder.'

'I was twenty yards or more from the pavvy and during the comings and goings I heard a few rather rich things.'

'We can't have that! Any names?'

'And although I disapprove of swearing in any form I did have some sympathy. The thing is, John, the boys spend all day looking forward to their afternoon game of cricket, you know what boys are like about their games, always whitening their boots and coating their bats with linseed oil, and then as soon as a bowler appeals you go and give the batsman out.'

'But that's what umpires do, isn't it?'

'Well, they can also give the batsman not out. In fact they usually do. Many umpires are by nature not-outers. And remember that howzat, which is a shortened form of how is that, is simply the bowler's appeal to the umpire for a judgement. Howzat or How Is That is a question to the umpire, that is all.'

'That's all it is?'

'I'm afraid so.'

Hearing snatches of this on the breeze, the fielders again started moving slowly closer, like a threatening herd of cows. The long-haired poet said firmly,

'I've had a brilliant idea.'

'Yes?'

'*You* can umpire, Miss Hoskins.'

'Me?'

'Yes, I'm in awe of what you know.'

'No, I'm not sure me taking over in the middle of a game would be good for you in your position. I have no wish to undermine you.'

He started to unbutton his white umpire's coat.

'But I am *asking* you to take over. Then I can sit on the boundary and watch you and learn. I can see that you know how to ginger them up. Miss Hoskins, you're a force of nature. You're a natural. What do you say? Here, you can borrow my umpire's coat.'

He took it off and held it out for her with theatrical courtesy.

'Oh, all right. As long as you help by keeping the scoreboard going. That'll be your job at the end of each over. And please make sure you acknowledge all my signals.'

'Oh, do wave to me as often as you like.'

'Just a moment,' she said, training her blue eyes on the boys, 'let me deal with this lot first. Back you go, all of you, Mr Betjeman and I are still deciding whether or not to allow this game to continue. If there's one more squeak out of...'

The boys retreated at speed but with the hint of a squeak. As they did so he admiringly helped her on with the umpire's coat. Her chest looked quite superb.

'Excuse my asking, John, but have you ever played cricket?'

'Oh yes I have played cricket.'

'How often?'

'Just the once.'

22 | IN THE HEADMASTER'S STUDY, 1928

The summons, half expected every morning, was not long in the coming. There it was, the note, lying in his pigeon hole in the Masters Common Room. It held his eye. Then he grabbed it and gulped his tea, finished his doughnut and, still licking the sugar off his lips, set off down the corridors for the headmaster's study, passing the butler and the housekeeper en route.

He was sweating. The last thing he wanted to be doing in the headmaster's presence was sweating. Fumbling with his left hand in the right sleeve of his jacket, he drew out his big spotted handkerchief like a conjuror and wiped his face and his moist hands.

After being made to bide his time like a naughty boy, like a naughty assistant master, he knocked on the door and went in and smiled a nervous smile, more a facial twitch than a smile, and faced the headmaster across the wide wooden floor. At the headmaster's feet lay Rex, his droopy old Labrador, chin on the carpet, dribbling, out for the count.

'Do sit down, Mr Betjeman.'

He sat on the upright chair confronting the large desk, crossing his legs, quickly uncrossing them and then finding he was crossing them again. *Sit still!* he said to himself in his father's voice.

'Mr Betjeman.'

'Yes, Headmaster.'

'We've already talked about all this. Yes, have we not, this important business? Yes?'

'What important business, headmaster?'

'Your teaching.'

'Ah.'

'Your methods. If methods they are. The turmoil in your lessons. Your... tone.'

'We have, Headmaster.'

'And yet here we are, here you are rather, sailing too close to the wind yet again, Betjeman. Far too close to the wind. A boy in your class has just been to see me. Well, he came along yesterday to see me.'

'Did he, Headmaster?'

'He did. And I have been sleeping on what he had to tell

me. Before I make a big decision on something, Mr Betjeman, I always sleep on it.'

John uncrossed his legs and leant earnestly forward.

'And which little... boy would that be, Headmaster, the boy you were talking to?'

'The boy Stevenson.'

He sat back, smiling.

'Oh, *Steve*-enson! For a moment I was a little bit worried there, Headmaster.'

'Were you?'

'Stevenson, this would be the boy who flicks peas in the dining room, the same boy cook pointed out to me only yesterday as, in cook's words, the one to watch, the very boy who does not accept that the umpire's verdict is final. *Steve*-enson. Yes, I know the one.'

The headmaster took off his spectacles, rubbed his eyes, and stood up to his full height very slowly, and rocked back and forward on the soles of his feet, a sequence which was not reassuring. He was, in his own weary way, lining up the artillery.

'We are not talking cricket, Betjeman, though I yield to no one in my love of the game. He came to me about your lessons. And repeated things which were said in your classroom which might have been, indeed would have been, better left unsaid.'

'Ah.'

'I am, in the broadest sense, Betjeman, please believe me, keen to offer you the fruits of my experience in schools, my thirty years experience in schools.'

'Thank you, Headmaster.'

'And, in that spirit, I have been wondering, what is your aim... during the time you are with us?'

'My aim, Headmaster?'

'Apart from survival, that is.'

Ah.

He decided to take his time on this one, as it felt a decisive moment. It was important that he appeared to be giving the headmaster's question his fullest and most undivided attention. To buy some time he looked at the framed photographs of school teams covering all the walls, at the mantelpiece chock-a-block with fixture cards, at a wicker basket brimming with shooting sticks and croquet mallets and hockey sticks and cricket bats, he looked at the comatose Rex, and last of all he looked at the headmaster's bald head and then into the eyes which lay beneath it.

'*Haw-haw-haw.*'

From a room deep within the private side, far beyond the green baize door, came that laughter, laughter he could now recognise anywhere, the laughter of a mad woman, that neighing like a war horse which was the signature tune of the headmaster's wife. She was always going haw-haw-haw. Imagine being married to that. You'd have to kill her, wouldn't you? Out of kindness. Oh, darling, there you are, you would say as she reappeared in your study, haw-haw-hawing, and you would open the bottom drawer of the desk, and reach in for the revolver, and bang! The thought of firing the bullet softened him somewhat and he found he was not all that far from looking sympathetically at the headmaster, given the lifelong burden he carried.

And the headmaster was right, of course he was, there was no argument, he *was* sailing too close to the wind. He always did, and he suspected he always would. As a little boy, on his Trebetherick holidays, he found that he enjoyed walking along the very edge of the cliffs, with a sheer drop and his mother's voice anxious on the wind and sudden death only a slip away to his left.

'John! Come back from the edge. John!'

'He's all right, Bessie. That's what I like to see, a bit of courage. Don't fuss the boy!'

'*Haw haw haw!*'

Then, somewhat to his own surprise, while looking at the

suntanned scalp of the headmaster, he heard himself saying,

'In so far as I have an aim, Headmaster, it would be to replace the games-mad snobbery of this place with creative writing snobbery.'

23 | MR T.S. ELIOT

Where was I?'
No answer.

He looked round the class.

'*Byes*, where was I? T.S. Eliot, yes. T.S. Eliot was the cat's whiskers then and he is now, T.S. Eliot was the topic then and he is now. He was tall and pale and he wore horn-rimmed spectacles. And he still does. And the thing was, the word got round Highgate Junior School, where I was for a while, that the old boy from Missouri was a bit of a poet, and as I myself was a bit of a poet, albeit a little younger – I was nine years old at the time – I gave him a copy of *The Best Poems of Betjemann*. A fair copy in my best copperplate, inscribed on the fly-leaf.

'It's very pleasant, as you would imagine, seeing one's name in print, or at least inside a cover with multi-coloured capital letters in crayon. My first book, even by the standards of most collections of poetry, was a pretty slim volume, but the American master, the old boy from Missouri, graciously accepted the gift from my hand, though I have to add that I am still not absolutely sure what he made of my poytry because he has never said a word about it from that day to this. Not a dicky bird. Probably because it was bilge.'

'What's bilge, sir?'

'Stale water in a boat, bilge water, hence filth or rubbish.'

'So your poetry is rubbish, sir?'

'Is my poytry rubbish? Well, my juvenilia is not my-best-wark-doncha-know. Anyhow, I'll give you a clue on the spelling of his surname. It is the same spelling as George Eliot's, George Eliot the novelist, who wrote *Adam Bede*, *Silas Marner*, *Mill on the Floss*, and *Middlemarch*, and who was, of course, as you all know, a woman. And when I say 'as you all know' I do of course realise that you don't.'

'Is that sarcasm, then, sir?'

'Yes, I suppose it is. Saying the opposite of what you mean could be construed as sarcasm. Fair point. My dear old top, do forgive me if you feel my remarks are of that order. If a fat chap comes last in the junior steeplechase and you shout out "Well run!" as he wobbles his way towards the line, you're being sarcastic, no doubt about it. At best, though, I prefer to see my words not as sarcasm but as a kind of gentle English irony, at worst as a rather tiresome schoolmaster's tic, an occupational hazard, a habit you catch, but it's a tone that seems to amuse we beaks. Anyway, it is odd, isn't it, to call yourself George Eliot when you're really Mary Ann Evans from Nuneaton, but dear old George Eliot *was* a bit odd, as well as looking like the back end of a bus, but probably no odder than most of us.'

'Do you have a photograph of her, sir?'

'No.'

'Do you like odd people, sir?'

'Oh yes, most of my friends are abnormal. Look no further than the poet Wystan Hugh Auden, who is coming to meet you again next week. Or, look no further than the novelist Arthur Evelyn St John Waugh who has just published a jolly funny story called *Decline and Fall*. I mean, what kind of names are those for chaps? *Wystan* and *Evelyn*. They could be the names of a music hall duo, a him and a her, couldn't they, or they could be two characters in an Oscar Wilde play. Good friends of mine though they are, and we were all close chums at Oxford, let's just say that Wystan and Evelyn are pretty rum individuals and a pretty rum couple together when they're a bit squiffy and leave it at that.

'The point I'm trying to make to you, *byes*, is that it is normal among my acquaintance to be odd. No one is less of a philosopher than I, but what percent of normal do you have to be, do you think, to be called normal? No, no, do forget I said that.'

He stepped down off the dais.

'The truth is, boys... I've made rather a mess of my life so far, but it's been the most enormous fun being with you, it really has, and whatever fools you make of yourselves in your later lives, remember, before you trudge off to the tomb to meet your Pilot face to face, it's better to be a mess than to join the mean and the spiteful and the ungenerous. It's the heart that matters. Honour thy father and thy mother. And do say your prayers.'

A boy's hand went up.

'Yes.'

'Have you been sacked, sir?'

'What makes you think I've been sacked?'

'The look on your face, sir.'

'The funny way you're talking to us, sir.'

'You're a laugh, sir.'

'I shall take that in the spirit in which I hope it was intended. Because with me people often don't know whether to laugh or not.'

'We don't want you to be sacked.'

'You are very special boys and as you are very special boys here is a very special question for you before I go.'

There were widespread groans.

'Do we have to, sir?'

'Ready? Apart from the fact that they're all characters in Shakespeare, yes Shakespeare, what do the following people have in common? Shylock, King Lear, Brabantio, Prospero and Henry IVth? Take your time. No hurry. Anyone? Oh I can't hang around all day waiting, I have to join Miss Hoskins in the gym. And the answer is Shylock, King Lear, Brabantio, Prospero and Henry IVth were all fathers who had trouble with their children. Tinkerty-tonk. Now *scram*!'

PART TWO

IN THE STUDIO

24 | EVERYONE AND NO-ONE

There were no trains.

There are no trains.

The 7.22, the 7.31, the 7.42 were all cancelled. Due to the weekend engineering work overrunning, there are no trains from Tonbridge to London today, none to Charing Cross and none to Cannon Street. Southeastern apologise. They are sorry. I looked up at the departures board one more time to be sure and then I asked a random passenger, as I tend to do, if there really were no trains to London. Looks like it, doesn't it, she said, her eyes flicking up at the board, with perhaps a hint of can't you read.

So, today of all days, I am going to be late. I hate being late. I have a bit of a problem with it, you could say, because I was brought up believing it was bad to let people down. Letting people down, particularly by being late, was casual and off-hand, if not downright arrogant. We Smiths prided ourselves that we were the sort of people who were not late. And to be on the safe side this morning I had allowed myself a generous two and a half hours for the journey to Maida Vale in West London, a journey which should normally, whatever that means, take no more than ninety minutes door to door.

Well, I am not going to make the ten o'clock read-through, which means they will either start without me (which is embarrassing) or they will sit around in the MV6 Green Room and drink BBC coffee and swap anecdotes and look at their watches and wait for the writer to turn up (which is embarrassing). Either way I am off on the wrong foot.

That it is not my fault is not the main point. Mind you,

to be honest, I did not go online to check if the trains were running, which – familiar as I am with Southeastern's track record of sending you round the houses – I could have done and should have done. So I was being casual if not cavalier, but still some way short of arrogant.

*

For a writer, the read-through with professional actors is quite a moment. For months, in this case years, the voices of all the characters have been speaking inside my head. For years I have been men and women, young and old, middle class and working class and upper. I have been outside my story, trying to shape it, and inside my story, living with them, both a player and a spectator, both attached and detached, *la plaie et le couteau*, a divided self running every run with them and bowling every ball.

But it's more than just being *in* a story and being *with* them. Because I have, as Jorge Luis Borges once described Shakespeare, been everyone and no one. Look no further than this story: I have been John Betjeman, I have been Ernest Betjemann (his father, and spot the spelling), and Bessie Betjemann (his mother). Soon I am to be Penelope or The Propellor, (his wife), Elizabeth or Feeble (his mistress), and that's not counting Archibald Ormsby-Gore (his teddy bear who never wet the bed) and the prefect thrashing the young Betjeman's backside at Marlborough College.

Bend over, Betjeman.

Bend over, Benchman.

Or is it Benjamin?

Whichever it is, whatever you're called, bend over.

I mean, the thing about being other people, about becoming other people, is: how many people can you pretend to be, how many skins can you inhabit and still be yourself?

Anyway, I have sat, 3B pencil in hand, in my hut in the

corner of the garden, scribbling away on a lined pad, with my handwriting getting smaller by the day, with only a charm of goldfinches for company, but aware that these exquisite little birds are drawn not by their love of me but of the nutritious niger seeds I put out.

Then I have crossed the small patch of lawn from my hut into the house to sit in front of my computer. Here I speak all the lines out loud, speak the speech I pray you, including the stage directions, reading first this draft, then that draft, doing rewrite after rewrite, tightening the dialogue, cutting it to the bone, telling myself less is more, telling myself that every page must have a surprise, always reminding myself of the power of gaps, and only very occasionally fleshing a speech out a bit. By the way, as a rule of thumb, cutting lines is good, adding lines is bad.

During these solo performances I have tried out lots of different accents, some of them comically off-key. You should hear me. I whisper and I shout and I stand up and I sit down, only to stand up again. I enjoy all the conflicts, adding (where need be) my amateur sound effects (*vroom vroom* for a car, *bam* for a slamming door, *mmm-wuw* for a sexless kiss, *cre-ee-eak* for a night-time door, *ring ring* for a bicycle bell, *chuff chuff toot toot* for a train), and I'm always checking my watch, always keeping one eye on the overall running time.

For a long while the whole operation has been all me. It has been private and personal. I have spent years on this 'project' – a word I don't like – on this *obsession* is closer to it, trying to be Betjeman, even to the point of getting the Parkinson's he had, doing my best to be inside his shoes and his head and his heart, which is no easy thing with anyone at the best of times but particularly tricky with John Betjeman. So I must feel there is still something new to say about him – even though he is a poet whose work is infamously intelligible.

Once the final script is accepted by the director, once we

arrive and gather at studio MV6 (preferably on time for the ten o'clock read-through), it is all mine no longer because I have, however quietly, gone public. My name is on the front page, that's true, but as with any novel or script, once you have 'put it out there', once you have raised your head above the parapet, they can all take a pot shot at you. And long before the critics do, you must see and hear what the director and the cast will come up with. What will they make of it all, what will they turn it into? Will it be faithful to my vision, or approximate to it? Will it be a better vision, or a worse?

Well, as Philip Larkin said of old age and death, we shall find out.

25 | FUMBLING FINGERS

At least we were now on the move, albeit on a bus, a replacement bus, a steamed-up double-decker full of fuming commuters, mostly busy on their mobiles. I'm going to be late. Very late.

Oh, no.

My left arm has started to play up, started to tick, then to feel hot. Here we go. Now it is pulsing. In an attempt to head things off, I try to reach with my right hand into my back right trouser pocket. I take out, or try to take out, the small laminated card I always carry with me. It is the size of a credit card. It is the card which lists my strategies, the questions to ask myself if I feel myself spiralling down, which I can all too easily do and which I certainly am. But I can't separate the card from the banknotes, they're clinging together, my fingers won't work. My fingers are disobeying me. Bugger them.

I stand up. Excuse me. Sorry. Excuse me. I am going to walk. Yes. When I'm walking I may look odd but I'm OK.

But if I get off I will be even later for the read-through than I'm going to be already. And I'm still miles away. So, sit down. Stay where you are. I haven't come all this way in the last year to fall at the last hurdle, not that it is the last hurdle, in life there are always more hurdles, aren't there, always, they keep appearing, you can't run round a track without hurdles.

To regain some calm, I press my feet hard into the floor of the bus, harder, then I press my backside hard down into the seat, harder, and then I press my hands firmly together. Feet, seat, hands. Feel your feet through your shoes, try to feel the floor.

After some deep breathing, but with my arm still burning and trembling, I emailed Bruce Young, the director. With unhelpful haste an automatic out of office reply came bouncing right back. I phoned him and got his message service.

'Bruce. Jonathan here. I'm having a bad journey. I'm going to be late. Not sure how late. Sorry.'

Deep breath.

And another deep breath.

Because it's not the end of the world, is it, being late, there are worse things than being late, it's not a matter of life and death, and the great thing is we have Ben.

We have got Benjamin Whitrow to play Betjeman. I am so looking forward to seeing Ben again. We have spoken quite often on the phone in recent months, and we have emailed each other (not a skill that comes naturally to Ben), but even a telephone chat is not the same as actually being with Ben and enjoying his droll mischief and his subversive humour. He's special. As we both like cricketing analogies let's say Ben hits the ball like no one else. His bat makes a special sound, a sound you don't often hear. As an actor he hardly seems to hit it at all, yet it reaches the boundary and the spectators so easily. Like David Gower. How on earth do they do that? Timing, I suppose. Touch.

And, if it doesn't sound too grand, I did write the plays 'for' Ben because I have worked with him and admire him as an actor (for one thing, and it's a big thing, you never feel he is acting) and because I know he can do Betjeman. He 'gets' John Betjeman in the way he 'got' Mr Bennet in *Pride and Prejudice*, and the way he 'got' Justice Shallow in *Henry IV Part 2* at the Barbican in the late 1990s. He can *be* Mr Bennet and Justice Shallow and (I predict will be) John Betjeman better than anyone else because he doesn't push or press too hard. He allows the line. He steals up on you. Close your eyes and listen to his timbre and his pitch and the colour of his voice and you can hardly tell him and Betjeman apart. It's not a practised technique, it's a gift.

Like David Gower.

26 | MV6

There are seven sound studios in Maida Vale, the home of the BBC Symphony Orchestra. Black and white photographs of the conductors down the years decorate the reception walls: Pierre Boulez, Adrian Boult, Colin Davis, and, oh hullo, there's Sir Malcolm Sargent, I remember him, how smart he was, Flash Harry, how spick and span he was on the podium, as sleek as a seal on the Last Night of the Proms.

As well as providing for classical and pop music, there are studios for drama at Maida Vale, and, once out of the taxi and through security with my named pass pinned to my jacket, I was hurrying down the long, low-lit corridors. The Maida Vale corridors are so narrow it's not easy to pass someone shoulder to shoulder, which leaves an opening for some old-fashioned good manners, where you both step aside, *After you, Claude, no, after you, Cecil*, as the RAF pilots used to say when queuing on the runway before taking-off on their Second World War missions. *After you, Claude* was a catch phrase from ITMA.

The thing is, Jonathan, and I don't want to be rude here, but nobody these days knows about Claude and Cecil and nobody cares. Furthermore, to pick up that reference to the 1940s comedy 'It's That Man Again', a cult hit on the wireless, you would need to be over seventy, no, well over seventy, nearer eighty in fact, to have a clue. That's a pretty small audience. I know, I know, I'm talking to myself too much these days. It's becoming second nature. I'm doing it in the car, I'm doing it as I clamber over stiles on walks, pick your feet up, I've noticed it, don't shuffle, and in the house when it's empty, not to mention mumbling away during those unmanageable hours in the middle of the night. I have been one acquainted with the night. I have walked out in rain – and back in rain. I have out-walked the furthest city light.

You mean you talk to yourself out loud? Yes, and often when I go into the bathroom I turn and confront myself in the mirror and give myself a hate stare, an evil.

All of which goes against the mental health advice I have been offered in recent times. I first saw the letters G.A.D. upside down on the psychiatrist's notepad during my initial appointment with him one dark December afternoon. (Teachers, by the way, come to be good at reading things upside down, especially unwelcome things, e.g reading 'God I'm Bored' being scratched by a pupil on a front row desk). After asking me a few direct questions, and then listening to me trying to describe what was going on, the psychiatrist decisively wrote down the letters G.A.D, and wrote them in capitals. Then, nodding to himself job done – he had heard enough – he put his pen in his inside jacket pocket.

– I can help you, he said.

– I've got to write two plays about Betjeman. They've been commissioned. I've got to.

– Fine.

– But I can't.

– I can help you, he repeated.

If you can't cope and if you are diagnosed with an anxiety disorder, one on-going line of advice is not to give yourself a hard time. Telling yourself you're pathetic and a failure (not to mention pointing out the obvious that millions of people all over the world are having a far more terrible time than you) only helps to make things worse.

The idea is, the advice is, to be kind to yourself instead. At first you may feel superior or facetious if not dismissive about this word of advice (and especially the tone) because it all sounds a bit wet, doesn't it, a bit feeble, particularly if you're a bloke, because a proper bloke isn't kind to himself, when the going gets tough the tough get going, hell, I played rugby, and I like blokes' bands, I know about The Who, I like to go racing in the street with Bruce Springsteen. But you soon drop all that. Because you have to. Because the wheels are off and you know it. Because this isn't a macho game. Because you're going nowhere, except down. The dam has burst.

So, would you, would you talk to a friend in the critical, unforgiving way you are talking to yourself? No, you would not. If you talked to your friends the way you are talking to yourself you wouldn't *have* any friends, would you, so think about it.

And I did think about it. And I am still thinking about it, and I am trying not to gesture at myself from up in the pulpit, trying not to point the finger at myself, let alone preach at anyone else, trying to avoid giving myself an evil in the mirrors and shop windows I pass. But old habits die hard, especially compulsive ones.

Anyway, I was talking (silently) to myself as I was hurrying along the ill-lit corridors to MV6. In fact, no offence and *pace* Claude and Cecil, this Maida Vale place does feel very Second

World War. It feels 1940-ish, a step back in time, all locked doors and airless secrecy. It feels somehow underground even when it is not. You suspect there could well be Alan Turing code breakers still beavering away in here, all smoking cork-tipped cigarettes, with 1940s haircuts, and twin sets, and sleeveless Fair Isle jumpers, brilliant brainy men and women working round the clock to defeat Hitler.

Round another bend, up and down a long ramp, I passed the Ladies and Gents (must remember where it is, picture it as if you're coming from the other direction, take a mental photo, at my age miss no opportunity to have a pee), now turn right, up a few random back steps and with a bit of luck I should find the Green Room to studio MV6.

*

John Betjeman often came to Maida Vale. He loved places like this, as I do, creative places that don't show off about being creative, as opposed to those shiny open plan modern places that look creative and aren't. Betjeman loved sharing his enthusiasms off-air with the technical crews, and the studio managers loved him back because he listened to them, because of his persuasive warmth, because he remembered their names, a simple but important thing, it's much more than a courtesy, and he liked their jargon. More to the point, he was vulnerable, openly vulnerable in public, which is so winning, particularly with women.

If ever there was an accomplished performer on the airwaves, Betjeman was. He was a natural story-teller and anecdotalist. According to Candida Lycett-Green, his loved and loving daughter, he appeared on the radio over 700 times and on television nearly 500 times. He was, in this and other things, not only a lover of the past but ahead of his times, the first poet to understand and to exploit the power of television

– which kept him in vogue when you'd think he would be out of date – and won him an even wider audience, while at the same time earning him yet more contempt from the academic critics.

Never mind all that, those critics are long forgotten and we are still reading him, and today we are gathered here together not to bury him but to bring him back to life, with me putting words in his mouth, what a cheek, what a liberty, and with Ben Whitrow pretending to be him. Or, in a phrase which I prefer, Ben Whitrow, the actor, and Bruce Young, the director, and I will be doing our level best to pull off the impossible: to re-create John Betjeman.

I have, by the way, been to Maida Vale on many occasions to record plays but, believe it or not, it was only today that it dawned on me for the very first time what the letters MV stood for. As with many of my blind-spots this one may be hard to credit. Sometimes it is clear that I cannot see what is staring me in the face.

I stand outside the Green Room door. Will they like my two plays? I check to see if my laminated security pass is still on my lapel. It is. For the nth time that morning I check my watch. It is 9.58. Made it.

27 | THE CAST

Right, there's Bruce Young, the director, down from Glasgow.

-Hullo, Bruce. Sorry I'm late.

-Don't worry, you're not.

The Green Room, MV6, is even drabber than I remember. It's a bit like the sort of place you might have been taken during the Cold War to await interrogation. I look round. Can't see

Ben Whitrow. Check again. No Ben. Bruce Young sits down next to me.

-Ben's running late.

-OK.

-We ordered him a taxi but he says it didn't turn up.

-One of those days. Never mind.

-He's on a train.

I go round and shake hands with everyone. It is smiles and nods, no kissing, no hugs, as I've never met any of them before. I meet their eyes, actors' eyes that don't miss much, quick eyes, sharp eyes, questioning eyes.

Who's here?

Nicky Henson, who I've seen only a few nights before on television, in a documentary about *Fawlty Towers*. Sophie Thompson, who I've seen only a few nights before in *Detectorists*, such brilliant television, hullo Sophie, hi Jonathan, she's Emma Thompson's sister and must be sick of everyone reminding her, so you don't. On the other long sofa is Philippe Edwards, straight out of drama school. Hi, is it Philip or Philippe? It's Phil-*eeep*. And Gerard McDermott, he's amazing with voices, he can do anyone, as well as any accent.

I've worked out – it's not difficult – who is playing whom, Ernest and Bessie Betjemann, the Younger Betjeman, the headmaster, and coming in the door a fraction late are the three naughty 'schoolboys' (adult actors who can age down).

There was no need to be nervous. No need at all. It feels like a good team and I like being in a team, I'm a team player. I feel at home.

28 | BEN

That unmistakable voice:
-Sorry, everyone.
-Ben!
-What a shambles! I bloody hate being late.
-Never mind. Good to see you, Ben.

He's standing at the MV6 Green Room door, blinking, unwinding his scarf. He often wears a scarf, in all weathers, and I've noticed he often keeps it on when he's acting. He's peering round the room, script loosely in hand, recognizing Bruce Young and Nicky Henson and then he sees and hugs Sophie Thompson.

He swivels slowly. He looks rattled. He looks thin.
-Is Jonathan here?
-Yes, over here, Ben.
-Ah.

He nods to me and we do a little low-key wave but I'm not sure he's sure it's me. Perhaps I have changed. Perhaps my condition has changed how I look.

29 | INSIDE THE CUBICLE

It's a bit like being on the flight deck of an aeroplane, a small aeroplane, not that I ever have been. Yes, you have, a Dakota in 1973, in Africa. Oh, yes, that had slipped my mind. Anyway, in the control cubicle, in the creative cockpit, there are five people, each with a copy of my script and the recording schedule. They are separated from the acting area by a wide glass window. Through the glass these five can see and hear the actors.

In fact I can see Ben in his turquoise cashmere sweater,

scarf still on, still chatting away to Sophie Thompson. She's laughing. And I could, if I wanted to be sneaky, eavesdrop on their conversation. Is his voice just a little lighter, is he a little more breathless than I remember?

In the front row of the cubicle sits the panel operator, the senior member of the studio managers team, and he is the one in charge of the technical side of the production. The huge mixing desk at which he sits strikes me as impossibly complicated (but then it would: in recent decades I have always sold any car I've owned before discovering how the radio works). He moves the levels up and down, playing the thing like an assured organist, trying this and testing that, pressing lots of buttons, pulling out all the stops, and only then does he decide that everything is as it should be, so that he can say:

Green light coming, everyone.

If he's not happy with some technical issue he is the first to say so. Occasionally he swings right round to speak to the director, with whom he has to work in close harmony. Both need to be satisfied with a take, with the quality of the performance, to be sure that there are no script noises (the give-away sound of pages being turned) and no fluffs, before we move on to the next scene.

The thing is, you have to get things right, but you have to move on. You don't want to rush it, but nor do you want to get bogged down. It's a judgement. The recording schedule is demanding, as is the demand for technical perfection. That's all part of the creative tension.

Behind the panel operator, and a few feet up, sit three people in a row, all facing the actors behind the glass. The three are: the director of the play, his personal assistant, and the writer. In my experience the writer sits on the director's left, the director in the middle, with his PA on his right. Among any number of other things to do, the PA times the scenes with a stopwatch, so that the director knows if the play is spreading, i.e. coming out longer than expected. A play usually 'breathes' and expands as you move through the recording schedule. That's the actors bringing it to life.

The writer is only there at the director's invitation. You have to understand this. The protocols may be unstated but they are observed. It is not my place, as the writer, to tell the actors anything or to give notes. Of course, if the director turns towards the writer to ask his view, that is another matter:

'So, what do you think?'

'It's OK.'

'Only OK?'

'I think she might be starting the scene too strongly.'

'Really?'

'Just a feeling.'

'You think so?'

'Yes, I do. Pressing the line a bit.'

'And not leaving anywhere to go?'

At which the director might pop into the studio and have a word with the actor, all very gentle, nothing heavy, slipping in that suggested tweak, slipping in that note along the way. And the point will be taken. I am in awe of the actors, of how good they are, and how skilfully they adjust and change, in the subtlest of ways, their performances.

If the relationship between the director and the writer is good you have a huge advantage. It may possibly be based on working together on earlier productions – for example, Bruce and I have collaborated for eighteen years – which allows you to carry on a running critical assessment by a nod, a glance, a raised eyebrow, the shake of a head or a quick 'lovely'.

Sometimes, if I am feeling uneasy, I will suggest a cut or a trim to my script even when I have not been asked, even when we are in the act of recording a scene, because I think I can see a better or more succinct way of doing it, and, if I do, I will slide the amended version across in front of Bruce. I will do this without a word. He will glance at it, and nod or demur. As a rule, I try to speak as little as possible but, when I do, to make it count. I do not get into the director's ear.

After all, Bruce is the boss. Bruce is the skipper. It is his show. He has been on the case, on the Betjeman project, for a year or so: he backed my idea in the first place, he encouraged the proposal, he helped shape the outline, he got it commissioned, well, he got *them* commissioned, because we're doing two plays not one, fighting my corner for months against a lot of competition, and then he has to cast it. And what's more, and this is massive, when the wheels were off in my life and I could not cope, he postponed the production for six months.

The director speaks to the actors on the studio floor by pressing a button and we all have to be careful what we say when he is doing so. Some things you do not want the actors to overhear. e.g, me once saying to the director about an actor who would keep banging on about something, 'Just tell him to shut the fuck up and say the line.' (Only once, honestly.)

Behind these three people, and slightly above, sits the grams operator. He records the play, deals with the background *atmos*, e.g. the wind in the trees, the Atlantic waves, the Surrey birdsong or whatever, indeed all the sound effects. When I started writing plays for the BBC in 1980, it was reel to reel tape, then it was cds, now it's all on computers. I remember the days when the Spot SM poured water from a hot water bottle on to the floor to suggest someone being sick, and, a favourite of mine, slowly twisted a stalk of celery for a garrotting.

Finally, down on the studio floor, is the Spot SM. The Spot is there with the actors, often seen but not heard, moving furniture, changing the position of doors or mics, finding props, popping out to the grocer's for the celery, and arranging live sound effects 'on the spot'.

It goes without saying but it bears repeating: in a creative collaboration like a drama, the tact, the instincts, the mutual respect between these five/six people and their relationship with the cast is vital. All this is easier of course if you love the teamwork.

The play is often done in a rehearse/record mode.

The director and the actors rehearse a scene, then the director says, right, let's go for a take. It's usually two or three takes before he's happy, sometimes more, or, if things are tricky, any number. In between the takes Bruce often leaves the cubicle to have a word with an actor, to refine a point or suggest a nuance. I don't hear what he says on these occasions, for all I know it might be, look, guys, it's a crap play, we all know that, but let's do the best we can with it, right?

Bruce Young is a clear-thinking Scot, decisive and extraordinarily well prepared. He is talent plus hard work. He does not keep actors waiting. He does not waste time. He does not do waffle, he maintains the energy and presses purposefully on, ticking the scenes off but keeping a strong sense of the overall tone and shape. He does not wear his heart on his sleeve, he is often understated, but he brings out remarkable performances. And when he leans back and says 'That's good enough for me, I like it' he gives us in the cockpit a lift. We've all played our part for the conductor, for the leader of the band.

Sometimes, as I said, he turns to me, but more meaningfully, to check if I am happy with a line I have written. This might be triggered by an actor asking, in the nicest possible way, if the writer would mind considering the slightest of changes. In nine cases out of ten I accept the implied criticism. Something is clearly not working, something feels off-key, and it's my problem, and I amend or cut or re-write. I don't resent this or feel defensive. It's my job. After all, after all we've been through, I want these two plays to be as good as they possibly can be. I don't mind cutting my own stuff because it usually makes it better.

You have to be light on your feet. So you should be.

After the read-through, because we were already running late, we headed off for a quick lunch in Paddington Sports park, a ten-minute walk from the studio. In the park there's a sort of large cricket pavilion which does soup and toasted sandwiches. We could have gone down to the BBC canteen but the sound engineers Garry and Mike prefer to 'get out' of the cubicle and breathe the fresh air.

I can't see Ben anywhere. I did catch his eye, just about, as we left the Green Room but he made no welcoming gesture, no see-you-in-a-minute nod, or none that I could read. Perhaps he was still upset he was so late. More likely, he simply wanted some private space, some time to himself. Sometimes, during a production, it's easier for writers and actors to avoid the specific chat and the implied comparisons and the sub-text notes, and that can most easily be done by gently avoiding each other.

I walk over to the park, talking Betjeman, talking snobbery, falling into step with Philippe Edwards, who is playing the young adult John Betjeman. Beyond the railings two schoolboy athletes, one black one white, are sprinting neck and neck down the running track. They are brilliantly good. At the end of the straight, in what looked like a dead heat, they ease up and grin broadly at each other. On the other side of the track a small group of runners are settled into middle distance laps. At the far end someone is pole vaulting.

Philippe has leading man good looks. He told me his father was an English and drama teacher, much as I was, and that he himself had just finished at LAMDA. Before that he was at Exeter University. This was his first radio role.

We talked about Betjeman's brief time as a schoolteacher, and would he have been any good, would the fun in class have outweighed the chaos, and then he asked me, as people often do,

'So, you reckon he was a snob?'

'When he was young, yes. That's the evidence.'

'And deceitful?'

'That's what his father called him. It's in *Summoned By Bells*. But we are deceitful at times. Well, I am.'

'So Betjeman levelled the accusation at himself?'

'Effectively, yes. He accused himself a great deal. On all manner of things. Perhaps he was rather good at guilt. Sometimes I think he enjoyed it, the guilty bit. On the other hand he can come across as comically breezy.'

'Is that convincing?'

'Probably a front. Look, I'm not sure, and I'm happy not to be. Perhaps he's leading us a dance, as writers like to do. Alan Bennett said something along those lines somewhere, but Betjeman seems riddled with shame all right. And remorse. I suspect a lot of us are. Underneath. It may be a matter of how long you can sit on it, before the chickens come home to roost.'

That the young Betjeman was a social climber is not in doubt. He was a North London suburban boy, a mummy's boy, an only child from a family with some money, they were well off, albeit with money made from trade, and he wanted to get on, and move up in society almost as much as he wanted to be a poet. The two went hand in hand.

He went to a famous school, Marlborough College in Wiltshire, but wished he had been to an even more famous school, Harrow in North London. Indeed, as a middle-aged man, he liked to don a Harrow hat (a boater to you and me) and he sometimes wore a Harrow Ist XI sweater. He made a joke of all this, as he did of so many touchy topics, inviting a laugh, but it says something.

From Marlborough he went up to a distinguished college at Oxford University, Magdalen College, but he soon worked, or clowned, or dazzled, his way into an even more social set, an even more exalted circle, the landed country house scene at the most powerful and established of all Oxford colleges, Christ Church, often called The House. Pronounced *The Hice*. Tom Tower, Peckwater Quad, the great dining hall, the Cathedral, the Meadows, a college later to be chosen as settings for *Brideshead Revisited, Alice in Wonderland, Harry Potter* and *Northern Lights*.

For Betjeman fans the question still hangs uncomfortably in the air. Doesn't all that social pushiness put you off? Yes, but then I'm put off by the private lives of so many creative people. And there's so much more to him, warts and all, so many qualities and strengths, generosity of spirit, originality, drive, warmth, kindness, but yes, the class issue, the pronunciation issue, there is no getting away from it, it is the less appealing part of his picture. Calling it *goff*, for God's sake, not golf. It's an earlier pronunciation, goff. Eighteenth century. That's Betjeman's persona, his game, his satire, looking for a laugh, showing off, or showing *orf*. How you speak, where you're from, where you live, where you 'went', all that is part of England, part of our comedy and certainly part of our tragedy. Don McCullin, the photographer, shows us all that. And it's still going on, all of it, still going on. The class affectations change, the class distinctions change, the class details change, but class in one manifestation or another is never far away, and always finding new forms.

Philippe and I order two soups and rolls. What's the soup? It's courgette. We'll have two of those.

We find a table and, happy to do so, talk about something else, the cricket, match-fixing, the football, the *Girl from the North Country*, the latest TV and film. What I don't bring up, don't admit to, is that my mother wanted my brother and me to go 'up in the world', up (if you like) from lower middle to middle. Not that we ever used those terms in my family, or even talked about the topic. She kept such things quietly to herself. But it was there, always there, always unspoken, and 'bettering ourselves' was what she was bent on doing, how you speak matters, speak properly, hold your knife and fork properly, your way of sitting at table, don't swing back on your chair, please and thank you, pass the pepper and salt, even if doing all this meant moving away from your family roots in the railways and the mines.

She did not much like rough people, my mother. She did not like the fact that her father drank too much of his money away at the pub as he walked home from laying the track. Think D.H. Lawrence, think *Sons and Lovers*. She thought one of her brothers, also a railway man, also a pub man, was 'rough and red-faced' and smelt of cider. And, in return and for good measure, one of my aunties thought my mother was a bit stand-offy, with a few airs and graces, in fact a bit of a snob.

If, in her last years, when she was sleeping downstairs, surrounded by her favourite pieces of furniture, but barely sleeping at all, listening to the soft tick tock of the grandfather clock, do sit and talk to me, Jonathan, if I had ever brought up all this class background stuff and pressed her, which I didn't, she would have said don't we all want to do the best we can for our children. It's natural, isn't it? I think it's right, don't you? Don't we all want to better ourselves?

And she certainly did her very best for me, every day of her life. When it came to me, nothing was too much for her.

My father, by the way, was a member of the National Union of Teachers. He was a grammar school boy, Porth County, in the Rhondda Valley. His father was a miner and, later, a cobbler.

I first met Ben Whitrow in 1985, well before he became Mr Bennet in *Pride and Prejudice*. I had asked him down to my home in Tonbridge to talk about acting to a group of my friends, all of them teachers and colleagues, inviting him in the belief that teachers can learn a lot from actors. Those dreaded in-service training days should always, in my view, include some time on stage. On one level, and a very important level, teaching is acting so why not learn from those who can act?

In the early 1950s, by the way, Ben had been a boarder at Tonbridge School with the two 'boys' who wrote Lindsay Anderson's film *If...* – and Tonbridge was the school where I taught English from the 1960s to 2002.

In his talk to us Ben was hilarious and frank and droll, talking freely about stage and film and television. Late in the evening someone asked – and this is the moment that sticks with me – what did he do if he found he was being directed by someone who was clearly no good. As an actor what could you do if, for example, you could see a better way of playing a scene, or a better set of moves? Ben nodded and smiled as if he knew the question was coming, and he stood up and glided around the room, with such quick feet, and such a quick mind, conscious of everything while remaining unself-conscious:

'Well, I might say something like this. "Sorry, I've just had a silly idea. What if, no, no, it won't work, but, this is off the top of my head, what if, what if Alison moves there and says her line, and what if... we move this chair from here to there, and then we both go on talking without looking at each other, no, it won't work, forget it. I'm sorry." '

At which the director, seeing it would unlock the moment and make everything a country mile better, would say 'No, Ben, that might work, that might work quite nicely. Let's give it a go.' In an almost apologetic way, and this was characteristic of Ben, he had subtly but adroitly avoided a shambles without humiliating the director. This is the same kind of game that teachers sometimes have to play, correcting a pupil without seeming to do so, without putting anyone down.

On stage, in 1983, I had seen Ben in *Noises Off*, playing the lead. I saw him as Thomas Cromwell to Charlton Heston's Thomas More in *A Man For All Seasons*.

The performance I can still recall in great detail, however, was his toothless Justice Shallow in *Henry IV Part 2* at the Barbican in 2000. Ben had, bravely, taken his front teeth out and he sat with Justice Silence (Peter Copley) on a bench downstage, his voice whistling a little. He brought the house down. After the show we had a drink in his dressing room and I thought what fun, *wot larks, Pip*, what a joy it would be to have him one day in a radio play of mine. Three years later he was.

In 2003 he was cast by Bruce Young as Winston Churchill in *The Last Bark of the Bulldog*, a drama about the cover-up of Churchill's stroke in 1953, a story which later became *Churchill's Secret* with Michael Gambon on ITV. Ben was Churchill on radio for a second time in a *A Portrait of Winston*, a play about Clementine Churchill's infamous burning of Graham Sutherland's brilliant portrait. This production was special for me because it brought together Ben and Dan Stevens, who I had taught at Tonbridge in the late 1990s.

While I was writing the Betjeman plays 'for' Ben I did something I would never usually do. I spoke to the actor before he was even cast in the part. And Ben would quickly ring back with a suggestion here or there, something apparently small, but a play is all small moments, often to do with more natural phrasing or allowing a gap or allowing a breath. He always helped words come off the page, and being told, by actors I respect, that my dialogue 'comes off the page' makes me feel ten feet tall.

★

In 2011 Ben came back again to Tonbridge, this time to make a short film with me. Before we started filming we went for a walk round the school, for old times' sake, right round the grounds, round the cricket field, and he reminded me that in the summer of 2003 we had spent a day at the St Lawrence ground at Canterbury, and were lucky enough to see Ed, my son, make a decent score, a hundred for Kent. We had a nice sunny day out on the green plastic seats, eating our smoked salmon sandwiches. The good days in cricket, when batting looks easy, are all the sweeter for being rare.

At Tonbridge we sat on a wooden bench, two grandfathers sitting under an after-storm sky, looking across at the chapel, and for some reason we came up with Betjeman's habit – we were talking about him even then – his habit of counting his cherry stones not as rich man, poor man, beggar-man, thief, but as church, chapel, agnostic, free thinker.

We talked about our sons and our daughters, and the sixth age and (rueful smiles here) about getting older. Nothing stops that. And we asked ourselves the question which comes up in an Anthony Powell novel: is it better to love somebody and not have them, or have somebody and not love them? And we talked about what matters in life and what doesn't, knowing one's fallible, seeing through the shoddy, about the great pleasure of being with gloomy people, about missing the bus, about nearly making it, keeping a light heart, and the froth of fame. And that's the kind of talk I love. It deepens my day.

'Ben, tell me about your time at Tonbridge.'

'Oh, I must have already.'

'No, you haven't. Not really. I've only imagined it.'

His eyes lit up but he paused, lost in private recollection.

'Well, I was naughty.'

'My imagination had risen to that.'

'I couldn't help myself. A bit like sex, I tried to, but, like ungovernable lust, I couldn't stop talking back to masters.'

'Really?'

'In their own voices.'

'Oh, dear.'

'I know. Asking for it. But I was good at it, good at their voices, good at asking for it. It became the main feature of the lesson.'

To give me a taste of it, he 'did' a few of his masters from the 1950s, masters I had never met, and they re-appeared and stood there in their academic gowns, re-created, chalk and board rubber in hand, brought back to life right before my eyes, the poor devils, only to be mercilessly mocked.

'Each day,' Ben went on, 'the class were ready and waiting at the ringside, willing it to happen, and I would oblige. I was the court jester. One master, when he was hopping mad, would say, and he would emphasise each word, "Up with this I will not put." And I'd put my feet up on the desk, with slow arrogance, one foot at a time, and say, "Sir, up with what in particular will you not put?" And that was it. Off to the headmaster.'

'Love it.'

'Always acting, anything for a laugh.'

'Like Betjeman?'

'Absolutely. Oh, not you again, Whitrow, the headmaster would say as I went into his study for another beating. What is it this time? I've been cheeky, sir. Have you, Whitrow? Dear oh dear. Better get on with it. Whack, whack, whack.'

'Did you resent it?'

'What?'

'The beating.'

'God, no, I deserved it. I was beyond a joke. I made some masters' lives an absolute misery.'

'Pitiless, that's the young.'

We stood up, warmed by our talk, and resumed our walk

round the school, past the pavilion, past the fives courts, then across the quad, into the classrooms, opening doors, looking into the same old places, gosh nothing's changed, well it has and it hasn't, it does and it doesn't, places you could find your way round blind-fold.

We went into the rooms in which B. Whitrow sat as a boy, into his boarding house, no longer a boarding house, into the chapel where someone was practising on the organ, and on the way out, in the ante-chapel, we looked up at the memorials, at the long list of those killed in the two world wars, and then, finally, Ben stepped out onto the Big School stage (there was no theatre in those days), the stage on which, as a boy, he had been Shylock and on which, earlier, in a house play, he had played the avuncular Osborne in *Journey's End*.

Out of the blue, and when the camera was rolling, he asked me about homosexuality, putting his cat among the pigeons. I told him about a housemaster friend who was interviewing, or being interviewed by, a married couple who were considering sending their son to his house. The father was an old boy of the school but it was the mother, as is increasingly the case, who came up with the tough questions. One of her questions was, is there much homosexuality? Oh no, my housemaster friend said, playing this yorker with the straightest of bats, as far as I know that's a thing of the past. Oh, what a pity, the husband said, that's the only bit I enjoyed.

After we'd finished filming Ben asked me would I mind, if we had time, and if it wasn't too much of a bore, if he recorded the *Seven Ages of Man*, the speech by Jaques in *As You Like it*. He said it was something he'd like to do, thinking about the passing of time, being back at his old school and all that, before his shanks had shrunk too thin.

Would I *mind*!

Speak the speech, I pray you.

We went to the recording studio. He took off his overcoat

but kept on his scarf and sat down in front of the mic. He closed his eyes. He mouthed the first few lines of the speech silently to himself, then collected himself, and nodded.

Green light coming, Ben. Ready when you are.

He knew the speech, no surprises there, he knew the speech by heart, Mr Bennet did, Mr Ben Whitrow did, because a man in his time plays many parts, Shylock, Osborne, Camillo, Cromwell, Churchill, Justice Shallow, John Betjeman and the melancholy Jaques.

And no apologies for printing it in full:

All the world's a stage,
And all the men and women merely players,
They have their exits and entrances,
And one man in his time plays many parts,
His acts being seven ages. At first the infant,
Mewling and puking in the nurse's arms.
Then, the whining schoolboy with his satchel
And shining morning face, creeping like snail
Unwillingly to school. And then the lover,
Sighing like furnace, with a woeful ballad
Made to his mistress' eyebrow. Then a soldier,
Full of strange oaths, and bearded like the pard,
Jealous in honour, sudden and quick in quarrel,
Seeking the bubble reputation
Even in the cannon's mouth. And then the justice
In fair round belly, with good capon lin'd,
With eyes severe, and beard of formal cut,
Full of wise saws, and modern instances,
And so he plays his part. The sixth age shifts
Into the lean and slipper'd pantaloon,
With spectacles on nose, and pouch on side,
His youthful hose well sav'd, a world too wide,
For his shrunk shank, and his big manly voice,

Turning again towards childish treble, pipes
And whistles in his sound. Last scene of all,
That ends this strange eventful history,
Is second childishness and mere oblivion,
Sans teeth, sans eyes, sans taste, sans everything.

32 | BETJEMAN JOINS THE MAJORITY

Dear Lord and Father of Mankind,
As well as fathers and sons, Lord, I have yet again been thinking about something difficult and deep and possibly dangerous, something I normally draw a veil over, and I wanted, in a moment of peace and security here in chapel, to ask you for your guidance. It is about how we feel, or should feel, about men and women, about men *or* women, and to which we are drawn, or is it to both? At school, at Marlborough, as you know, it was all boys. At Oxford it was all men, or mostly men and a few jolly clever gels. And then the thing was, at Oxford, I found I liked quite a wide bunch, a generous range, and I found I changed week by week, if not more often. I was on shifting sand.

To put it plainly, Lord, I was confused, and I *am* confused. It's a hellishly ticklish business. Which camp am I in? When I'm with Wystan or Walter it's one way, they're my cup of tea, when I'm with Myfanwy or Margie they're my cup of coffee, and they're both jolly good fun. All of them. Does one have to be one or the other to know the meaning of passion? And what's more I sometimes am not sure, not at all sure, how many people I am myself.

I haven't hope. I haven't faith.
I live two lives and sometimes three.

The lives I live make life a death
For those who have to live with me.

★

In 1933 John Betjeman came down on the side of the majority because he not only kissed on the lips but married the horse-loving Penelope Chetwode, daughter of Field-Marshal Sir Philip (later Lord) Chetwode, Commander in Chief of the British Army in India. And you can imagine how much The Old Field-Marsh took to having a poet carry off his daughter. In an early interview he said to his son-in-law, 'So, Betjeman, what are you to call me? It can't be Philip, and it can't be father, I'm not your father, so let's settle for Field Marshal.'

The following year John's father died. He had a heart attack. The kind of heart attack they call massive. Bang. One minute Ernest was there with his ear trumpet, bang, next minute he wasn't. There were no good-byes. And, strangely enough, it was that one about the Bullingdon boys at Oxford, *The Varsity Students Rag*, the lightest of his poems, that touched the rawest of raw nerves with his father. That was the poem that led to their worst row, reprising as it did all the old issues, and it happened over breakfast down in Cornwall, in Daymer Lane, in the house where he had been so happy as a boy.

But that's nothing to the rag we had in college the other night;
We'd gallons and gallons of cider – and I got frightfully tight.
And then we smash'd up ev'rything, and what was the funniest
   part
We smashed some rotten old pictures which were priceless works
   of art.

Ernest must have been reading that verse just before his son came downstairs. It was lying open on his place at the breakfast table.

'What sort of time do you call this?'

John yawned.

'I'm afraid I can't say as I am not yet fully awake.'

'I didn't hear you!'

Ernest turned sharply towards his wife.

'*What* did he say, Bessie?'

'I wasn't listening, dear. Speak properly to your father, John. You've got a very nice clear voice when you care to speak properly. Speaking properly is very important in life.'

Ernest tapped the table with his knuckles.

'So I'll ask you again, young man. What sort of time do you call this?'

'Why not consult your watch, Father?'

Making a little pantomime of it all, his father put his hand into his waistcoat pocket, frowned, felt around and slowly produced his silver fob like a rabbit out of a hat.

'Oh, I will… Ah, let me see. So the budding bard is good enough to honour us by coming down at… ten past ten.'

'Would you like some bacon and eggs, John?'

'I didn't want to come down into this fug, only you started shouting at Mother and that put an end to my night. They could probably hear you on the beach.'

'Oh, John dear, I think that may be a tiny little bit of an exaggeration, don't you?'

'Who in his right mind would leave the warmth of his bed on his holiday to come down to all this? I was trying to read, I have a lot of reading to do, serious reading to do, but I had to give up.'

His mother put her hand on his.

'You'll help me with the weeding this morning, won't you? You did say you would.'

'Yes, all right, all right, I'll help you with the weeding.'

'No, he won't. He's cleaning the car first and then he will caddy for me this afternoon.'

'I damn well won't.'

'You damn well will.'

'Let's see if I do.'

'You're bone lazy. You will be obedient to me, by God you will. And stop fidgeting when I'm speaking to you.'

'Not now, Ernest, please. Not *again*.'

He re-lit his pipe, sucking deeply as he spoke:

'It's time he earned his keep, helped to pay his way. At his age I was up at dawn and working at the bench and getting on with the men.'

'Making onyx cigarette boxes covered in lapis lazuli?'

'Yes, and proud of them.'

'Making those ri-dic-ulous tantaluses! To lock the decanters away from the servants! What an achievement!'

'Yes, and that's how we have afforded to send you to the Dragon School and to Marl-bor-ough College. Money doesn't grow on trees, money's not easy to earn, but all you do is waste it. I'm beginning to feel that I have made a poor investment.'

'It's *Maul*-brough. Not *Marl*-bor-ough. I've told you, it's pronounced *Maul*-brough.'

'Listen to me –'

'*Maul*-brough. It's not difficult, and it's embarrassing you getting it wrong all the time. It's so coarse. I could see Patrick and Harry *wincing* when you kept mispronouncing it.'

'And when was that?'

'After church on Sunday.'

'Oh, wincing, were they?'

'And what's more I wish I'd never been near the place. *Maul*-brough, I mean, not the church.'

'What's wrong,' his mother asked, 'in trying to better ourselves? Will one of you please explain to me what's wrong with that?'

'Listen to me, you ungrateful little snob,' his father said, 'I'm in trade and I'm not ashamed of it, I'm proud of it.'

'Here we go.'

'You're the one who should be ashamed. You don't begin to understand that some men live rough so that some men can live smooth. You can be as hoity-toity as you like and think we're not good enough for you, that I'm too coarse for you and your grand friends, that you're a cut above, but the simple truth is you're not good enough for us!'

The son turned away from his father and towards his mother.

'Aren't there any kidneys?'

'They've all gone, dear, I'm afraid. But I'll get Bertha to do you some bacon and eggs.'

'I don't like bacon and eggs.'

'Oh, honestly, what is up with you this morning?'

'Especially when they taste of pipe smoke.'

'Everybody likes bacon and eggs,' his father said.

'I'm not everybody.'

'Oh, there's no need to tell me. I do know that, and that's the problem.'

'What is? What is the problem?'

'Stop it, you two! Please! Have a care. I've got one of my toothaches.'

'And earache, Mother, I should think.'

'I wish you *were* like other boys!' his father roared.

'Do you?'

'Yes!'

'Like other manly chaps? Oh, not *mens sana in corpore sano*, spare me.'

'You don't get your hair cut, oh no, not you, you visit old churches or lie in bed at all hours talking to your bloody silly teddy bear. You do everything for effect and you're not exactly partial to a day's work. It won't surprise me if you make a mess of your life. You went off the rails at school and you went off the rails at Oxford. Well, I've had enough of it and we're going to have a good talk, the two of us, because although you're my only son I'm not sure you're a boy at all.'

On the word 'boy' both his fists came down on the dining table and made the cups dance and the vases tremble.

'Stop it, *both* of you.'

'Keep out of this, Bessie!'

'No, I won't.'

'I said keep out of it.'

'You're *both* in the wrong!'

'Mother, I don't want any breakfast, thank you, and I'm going out because I don't feel at home here. One thing is very clear and I think I ought to tell you. We have nothing in common.'

His mother started to cry.

'John, John, that's the most terrible thing to say. If this goes on, you'll kill him. *And* me, you will. He's got angina. No one, no one can make us feel as wretched as you do. And he *is* your father.'

'More's the pity.'

Sobbing loudly, the mother hurried out of the room. The boy pushed back his chair. The father pushed back his.

'And another thing I've noticed, you're always more deaf

when mother is speaking.'

'What did you just say?'

'You heard. And what's more you haven't the faintest notion of what goes on inside my head.'

'Stay where you are, young man, and look me in the eye.'

'I don't want to look at any part of you.'

'Oh, don't you!'

'Just bugger off.'

'Did you say bugger?'

'Yes, I did say bugger.'

'Bugger is a most disgusting foul word and a most disgusting foul thing. Do you know what a bugger is? A bugger is a man who puts his piss-pipe up another man's back passage? Perhaps that sounds acceptable to you? Your sort of caper, is it? Look at me! You've let me down terribly. And you've let your mother down, because you'll always be second-rate, I knew it from the moment you were born. I said stay where you are, you've turned your back on the family and where you come from, you've turned your back on the firm and when I'm dead you'll be sorry.'

'Sorry when you're dead? Oh no I won't.'

'Come back, you vindictive little sod, you flibbertigibbet! If you won't carry on the firm I'll cut you out of my will. I will, I'm warning you. See if I don't! Right, I am cutting you off! John, come back here this instant!'

John ran like mad, like a madman, his eyes wild, his knee banging into the dining room door frame, then banging his elbow on the front door, he ran out of the bungalow and out into the open air, plunging down the lane, past the hissing geese, ducking through the bonfire smoke drifting over a hedge, and he ran towards Brae Hill, running just below the edge of the dunes, he jumped over bits of driftwood and piles of bladderwrack, and then he veered towards the roaring sea, past the boys and girls in shorts and shirts playing cricket and shouting to each other in the strong wind and the Scottish family damming and diverting a stream and his feet splashed in the warm shallow pools and then he turned back up to the dunes and he ran and gasped keep going don't stop keep going I hate him I hate him don't stop keep going and he ran and he gasped and he kept going up and over the dunes and across the fairway not caring if he was hit by a golf ball and past the edge of the 10th green and up the path to the church and left through the lych gate and sharp right up the steep graveyard until he slumped on the grass with his back to the lichened wall.

34 | PORTRAIT OF A DEAF MAN

The kind old face, the egg-shaped head,
The tie, discreetly loud,
The loosely fitting shooting clothes,
A closely fitted shroud.

He liked old City dining rooms
Potatoes in their skin,
But now his mouth is wide to let
The London clay come in.

He would have liked to say goodbye
Shake hands with many friends
In Highgate now his finger-bones
Stick through his finger-ends

You, God, who treat him thus and thus,
Say 'Save his soul and pray',
You ask me to believe
You and I only see decay.

After Ernest died the factory closed. And that was the end of Betjemann and Son. John was sorry about that and sorry about him. And even more sorry that he had painted him the way he did. Ernest was a decent man, and he couldn't answer back. The truth was, he disappointed him. Some fathers are disappointed in their sons. Some sons are disappointed in their fathers.

But you can't *make* yourself love someone, even your own child. He thought about that a great deal. Fathers and sons. My father and his son. As for him and his son, his son Paul, that was a story for another day.

PART THREE

35 | THE POET LAUREATE

I've often wondered how Betjeman reacted to, or dealt with, the onset of his Parkinson's. As far as I can find out, it began in the early 1970s when he was in his late sixties and a very popular public figure. When did he notice the first signs, the feet not responding, the difficulty swallowing, the loss of strength, the brain messages taking a bit too long to get through? Did it creep up on him? Was it a physical weakness or a pattern of clumsiness that could easily pass for the general indications of old age? Was there a day when he knew for certain that it had been triggered? And if so, did he manfully accept it or did it darken his melancholy, making his mood swings even more pronounced?

And, a low thought, was there perhaps the unspoken suspicion amongst his friends and family that he was playing the little old man, shuffling along more than he needed to, enjoying the doddery, playing the sympathy card, playing for laughs, indeed playing for both? I bring this up because some days I suspect my family suspect me of doing something similar, of crying wolf, oh, there's always something wrong with Dad, he'll be fine, don't worry about him, jolly him out of it, take no notice, look at him, you can't even tell he's got it. And, dammit, I do want to be thought strong, or at least not a complete wuss.

Well, I don't know how it went in Harley Street with the newly knighted Betjeman ('Well, Sir John, not too bad a report, things seem to be slowing down just a little on the circulation front, nothing too alarming on mobility, what? yes, of course you can have a glass or two, not too early in the day perhaps, keep your eye on it') but I do know how it came about with me, or I think I do.

Over the course of time when I was possessed by Betjeman, I had noticed I was bumping into doorways with my right shoulder, or clocking up near-misses with other pedestrians or (a new hazard, this) narrowly avoiding those bearing down on me in their motorised wheelchairs. I noticed I was brushing my elbows against walls, or, out on a country walk, finding the land surprisingly uneven, clipping the ground occasionally with my right foot. At the top of staircases, and Doctor Bruce this has absolutely nothing to do with the drink, I sometimes swayed and had, oops, to hold on to the banister. When it came to cutting up meat my right hand felt less strong and skilful, my grip on the knife less secure, which pisses me off, and when I was reading in bed the book once in a while seemed to tremble very slightly in my right hand, to have a mind of its own, a barely measurable interior movement on the Richter scale.

Finally, and this did it, I returned for a feast at St John's, my Cambridge college. Such occasions make it clear how many of your contemporaries have gone, and such occasions also require one to wear a dinner jacket, and I got into a terrible tangle with my bow tie, ending up with fingers on both hands strapped to my neck. Yet, believe it or not, when I made an appointment to see my NHS neurologist and told him all this, in what I hoped was a fairly entertaining way, I did not for one moment expect the diagnosis. Instead, I put all the above symptoms down to the ageing process, and dusting off my sort-of Yorkshire accent, I told myself *there's nowt funny, lad, about getting old.*

And when the consultant asked me in a very matter-of-fact way to do this or do that, to lift this, lower that, look this way, look that, eyes up, eyes down, press this or that, now just walk to the end of the corridor and back, would you, Mr Smith, I was thinking this is pretty easy, come on, I'm doing pretty damn well here, I'm taking all this in my stride, out of ten I'd say it's an eight or a nine, when do we get to the difficult bit?

So, when he said I'm afraid I've got bad news for you, I was not expecting it, I really wasn't. I must be what my father called a bit slow on the uptake, and knowing my face quite well, as after a lifetime I do, I felt myself taking a moment or two to absorb exactly what I had heard. In his follow-up letter a few weeks later, confirming the diagnosis of Parkinson's, (citing the reduced arm swing, the ipsilateral rigidity, the minor finger tapping), he wrote that this unexpected news, on top of Mr Smith's generalized anxiety disorder, was naturally a shock for him which of course shows that, even after a lifetime of its company, I do not know my face at all.

★

The old man makes his way slowly, painfully, up the steep, grassy churchyard, in sight and (nearly) in sound of the sea. You can see by the way the old man places his foot. That's Parkinson's. One foot, then (too long a pause) the other foot. Each small step a placement. You can see by the way his right arm hangs stiffly. It does not swing. He arrives at 'his' bench and sits heavily down, almost falling backwards as he does so.

If ever they want to interview him when he's in Cornwall, this is where he brings them, to the place to which he always ran as a child.

And, boy, do they do want to interview him in the 1960s and 70s. Because he's a household name and he's good at the chat, they'd interview him all the time if they could. For the telly, or the wireless, or the Sunday newspapers. If the Poet Laureate isn't being filmed on a train or on Southend Pier or at Weston-super-Mare he is being filmed walking round a church, craning his stiff neck. Some days he feels he does very little else apart from look mournfully out of a train window or shuffle around a church, or (as it orften sounds) a *charch*, peering up and pointing out architectural features.

The fact, the sad fact is, he doesn't actually write many poems anymore. Now it's all Sir John this and Sir John that, which of course he quite likes, but it's not good for you, you know. Not good for the soul. You can easily end up being not so much a popular poet as a media tart, saying something quotable on chat shows, chat shows are money for jam, recycling something anecdotal, coming up with something along the lines of:

'Cornwall! You can't beat it, can you? I always say… a year in which one doesn't go down to Cornwall doesn't feel quite right.

What a view!'
(allowing the camera to pan the skyline slowly from left to right)…

'So, here I am, on my favourite seat, on my very own bench, at the top of Saint Enodoc churchyard. Amongst the tumbling tombstones, in Trebetherick. It's been said that I would rather take a woman to church than to bed… as long as it's the Church of England. Well, I've been coming here, man and boy, for, oh, well over sixty years now. If you look straight ahead, past the church and the crooked spire, there is the Atlantic Ocean.

'And when the wind's in the right direction, if you're lucky, you can just about hear the children playing cricket on Daymer Bay. It's where I played with my children. To my left, beyond the golf course, is Padstow. To my right is Polzeath, the famous surfing beach. I lost my bathers once in Polzeath. Terribly embarrassing. I had to walk out of the sea, eyes down, with my surfboard clutched closely in front of me, with my children, Paul and Candida, bringing up the rear.'

That's the sort of borderline naughty thing he can do on telly at the drop of a hat. Oh, he can turn it on. Still, as Larkin says, you've got to give them a bit to be going on with. The trouble is, Larkers old boy, they always want a bit more, don't they, about your private life, about your family, and most of all about me and Penelope and our marriage, and they're not going to get it, and certainly not about me and Elizabeth.

All this fawning and then all this sniping can drive you potty. You end up resenting both, especially when your life is reduced to looking at the pattern on the wallpaper by the bedside table, or looking out at the potting shed in the garden. You've been through so much, you've experienced the comedies and the tragedies and the histories and the tragic-comedies, and there are only the late plays left. And do, please, forgive the Shakespearean parallel.

But, whatever he says in his chats on the telly, every time he brings out a collection of poems, the academic critics, the literary intellectuals, reach for the knives. The clever dicks. The snipers. Oh, you know, just the usual stuff: Betjeman is no Eliot and no Auden. Instead of taking us forwards Betjeman is taking us backwards. For example, does one need any more Betjeman poems about Robertson's Marmalade and boys in Aertex shirts? Does one need any more poems about mountainous girls and subalterns and elderly schoolmasters in shorts?

One snipe in particular stays in the memory.

Betjeman is harmless enough. He is an intellectual fuddy-duddy, a poetic reactionary, a minor writer of middle class values. One might ask, where is the mind? Where is the depth?

That's what he gets. Because, as he often says to Feeble, they don't actually read his poems, they know about five or six of them, and as for the middle-class book-buying popularity he enjoys, that really sticks in the critics' craw. They're jealous of recognition.

No one in England likes a success.

He has, of course, committed the cardinal sin of clarity. The problem is that he's not difficult enough for the clever dicks, and they do like difficulty, don't they? They like poems they can be clever about, poems they can de-code or un-code before a class or in a lecture hall. And if the poets aren't difficult the academics are out of a job. Well, fuck them.

In fact, and whisper it not, it is easy to be difficult.

Anyway, he's up here, up in the churchyard, as he so often is, this is where he comes for warm chats with journalists and for severe talks to himself.

They know about *her*, about Elizabeth, of course they do, they know all about the daughter of the Duke of Devonshire, but nobody's saying. And they were not going to have a chance to say anything as long as he was *compos mentis*. Was he of sound mind, memory and understanding? Good question. As well as coming up here to do interviews he also came, on his own, to escape the voices in his head, the chattering monkeys, but you never can, you never can escape yourself, and the more you try to avoid thinking about Penelope and Paul and all that happened in the past the more it keeps coming up behind you, like bicycle bells in a country lane, move over, move over, let me pass, let me pass.

36 | A TIFF, 1933

There was a tiff. With Penelope there often was. Or, let's be kind, let's call it a little tension. Anyway, it was the first of many small clashes for the lively newly-weds, a sign of things to come between the poet and the Field Marshal's daughter, before they started to flounce out after a spat, before they moved on (pretty damn soon) to cutting each other down to size in brutal earnest.

'John.'

'Yes, Penelope.'

'I've been thinking.'

'Oh dear.'

'About where we're going to live.'

'I thought we'd agreed on all that.'

'Did we?'

'We did. A little flat in Chelsea would be just the thing, a nice place to start.'

'You think so?'

'Just orf the King's Road, in walking distance of Holy Trinity, Sloane Street.'

'Not sure we can afford that, even with Daddy's help.'

'Oh we can, we can, everything's going very well.'

'In what way is everything going well?'

'I've got a collection coming out.'

'Does that mean money?'

'What a nice way you have of putting it!'

'I can see Chelsea working for you, John, only too well, but I was thinking along different lines.'

'You were?'

'How about one of those villages in West Berkshire? Or Oxfordshire? Wiltshire at a pinch. That neck of the woods.'

'You mean right out in the country?'

'It's not as far as Cornwall.'

'Who's mentioned Cornwall?'

'You, you're always mentioning it. Cornwall this, Cornwall that.'

'Well, it's special, very special to me.'

'Anyway Berkshire's not right out. Places like Wantage or Lambourn are perfect, on the downs, with a station for London nearby. You'd like that.'

Her eyes were shining bright.

'Ah,' he said.

'What?'

'I can hear the sounds of hooves.'

'Can you!'

'I can hear the sounds of gymkhanas and goats. I can smell stables and mucking out.'

'Oh good!'

'You and your pony and a field and a fete in Faringdon.'

'You don't mind, do you? I bet you see it all as material for more poems.'

'Of course I don't mind, my darling. Even if I do sometimes think you love horses more than you love me.'

'That's a silly thing to say. They've always been a part of my life. I grew up with them in Injer. Let's at least have a looky, shall we?'

'We will, Penelope, we will. Anything you ask.'

She rushes over and kisses him on the cheek.

'On the Berkshire downs, I thought. And we'll need a lovely church, of course.'

'With a high church vicar. And incense.'

'Oh, that's a must. That's a given.'

'His Kingdom stretch from see to see
Till all the world is C of E.'

'And you'll be a churchwarden in no time, you'd love that, John, with all the locals whispering "That's the poet!"'

'And at Christmas we can do the Nativity Play together.'

'Bags me playing the cattle,' Penelope said.

'What a hoot!'

'I'd love to act with you, John. Because you're always acting.'

'Am I!'

'Just one thing, though.'

'Sounds ominous.'

'Before we do, someone's going to have to tell Daddy. That we're married.'

'Good point, yes. Good point.'

'Perhaps next weekend, would you?'

'All things considered, my love, I thought it might come

more easily from you.'

'From me?'

'Yes.'

'Isn't that a bit wet?'

'Talking of high church vicars.'

'Were we?'

'Did I ever tell you the one about *Onward Christian Soldiers*?'

'No.'

'With words by Sabine Baring-Gould?'

'No, you didn't.'

'He knew St Enodoc Church very well, by the way, Baring-Gould knew his North Cornwall like the back of his hand. But the old boy got into terribly hot water, you know, over the words.'

'Of *Onward Christian Soldiers*?'

'Yes.'

'How come? They seem sufficiently military.'

'Well, some of the low church lot didn't take to the line *With the cross of Jesus going on before*, they thought it altogether too papist, so he suggested he could always change it to *With the cross of Jesus left behind the door*.'

Penelope slapped her horse-woman's thigh.

'Priceless!'

Penelope and John had married secretly in Edmonton Register Office in 1933, not far from the prep school where he taught. The ceremony was followed by roast beef and Yorkshire pudding at the Great Eastern Hotel, Liverpool Street and a three day honeymoon in Essex. The wedding had not been announced between the middle class John Betjeman and the upper class Lady Penelope Chetwode, daughter of Field Marshal Sir Philip (later Lord) Chetwode, Commander in Chief of the Army in Injer. No need to ask what the Field Marshal thought of the secrecy or the haircut. Not the kind of chap to be found in the cavalry.

37 | A BIRTH IN UFFINGTON

That December, the December of 1937, was bitter on the Berkshire Downs, with blankets of frost, thick fogs and horses risking their footing on the black ice. Whatever you did, you could not escape the cold and the murk. It followed you on a walk, the cold, the cold, it followed you indoors. In their pew in Uffington Church on Sundays the noses of John and Penelope Betjeman were almost as red and their hands almost as blue as the reds and the blues on their kneelers.

> *A cold coming we had of it,*
> *Just the worst time of the year*
> *For a journey, and such a long journey,*
> *The ways deep and the weather sharp,*
> *The very dead of winter,*
> *And the camels galled, sorefooted, refractory*

Even though he had been out of bed for only fifteen seconds or so, tugging his dressing gown tightly around his ample stomach, he was already shivering. For a few moments he stood stock still in the darkness, waiting for his eyes to adjust, waiting to pick up the first dim outlines of the furniture. Above all he must not bang into anything.

With his hands stretched out in front of him like a pantomime ghost, he fumbled his way round the bedroom walls, bumping against the side table (piled high with books), touching the tall wardrobe with his fingertips and eventually locating the position of the electric light (but not, heaven forbid, switching it on). He could hear Penelope breathing deeply in her sore and exhausted sleep. Go gently. You woke The Propellor at your peril.

He turned the doorknob as slowly as he could so that there would be not the slightest noise. Not a sound. Then, as he opened it a foot or so, the door squeaked, and it felt quite a prolonged squeak. That's the trouble, the more you go around on tiptoe in the dead of night, the more you hold your breath, proceeding like a soldier picking his way carefully through a minefield, the more your feet seem to find the creakiest farmhouse floorboards, and the Betjemans had plenty of creaking floorboards in Garrards Farm, Uffington, Berkshire, telephone Uffington 46.

At two in the morning clocks tick more loudly.

At two in the morning you can hear your heart thrum.

You might well hear the high-pitched shriek of a fox's mating call.

Right, here I am.

And here he is.

John got down on one knee, as if genuflecting.

He looked over the side of his crib.

In a grateful haze he knelt beside his newborn son, beside his first child. There was barely enough light to make out his egg-shaped head and the line of his thin neck. The boy's miniature oval head — as John had noticed the very first time he saw him — was exactly the same shape as the boy's grandfather's. You could not see his eyes, and anyway they were closed and anyway it was dark, but John knew that they were blue... as blue as his own dead father's.

Paul was lying tightly wrapped against the cold, a little parcel, helpless, vulnerable, frail and tiny. How terribly tiny a tiny baby, his tiny baby, is. How close to death a baby is, wrapped in a blanket or a shroud.

There had been a birth, certainly.

John sat on the floor to be with him, and closed his eyes and strained to listen. They would breathe together, breathe in time with each other, father and son, heartbeat to heartbeat.

To love is to learn. He could hear his own breath all right but was the baby breathing? Shhh... was he? He was too quiet. John moved his head a little closer to his tiny mouth. Nothing. Not a breath. No, don't tell me that. No, it can't be, it cannot be. He wasn't breathing!

John got up on one knee and leant right over the crib until his ear was almost touching the baby's mouth, whilst barely breathing himself. Hold your breath! Was there not the slightest of sounds? Yes, there was. Then another slight gurgling sound and then the wave of relief and the rush of palpitations as he sank back to the floor.

Did other fathers do this?

The Propellor had a fearful time bringing the boy into this world, such a hard time of it, and such a long journey, with many hours of labour followed by a Caesarian, before Paul Sylvester George Betjeman was delivered in sight of White Horse Hill in the county of Berkshire on November 26th 1937. She told one of her friends that she wished 'It' could have been a little horse.

Talking of which, what annoyed Penelope the most in the last part of her pregnancy was their family doctor firmly advising her that she should not ride Moti, her Arab gelding, but instead should go about the place in a four-wheeled dogcart. This advice, firm though it was, she took very badly. If The Propellor had her way she would spend her whole life with horses, with stable smells, with saddles, in the yards, with professional jockeys in nearby Lambourn, watching the high-stepping greys, handling the harness, hearing the jingle, riding on the swelling downland and over her favourite fields, going up to the gallops and out to the gymkhanas. That was poetry enough for her.

And if it wasn't her horses it was her goat.

Which reminded John, he did see a horse go down that bleak winter, the only time he had ever seen it. It was a day or two before Paul was born. There was a passage of hooves outside their house, that special sound of a string of horses, and he heard a rider call out 'Go steady here, lads, this bit's a skating rink.' Sensing some drama might be coming, being a bit of a drama queen himself, John put down the book he was reading and moved to the window and watched the line of jockeys pass by, crouching slightly forward in their saddles, backs rounded, hands limp, like the hands of fishermen in anticipation of a sudden convulsion, and a second later there was indeed a terrible convulsion, as the last horse crashed heavily down, ripping up its knees. Fortunately Penelope was making some vegetable soup in the kitchen and missed the distressing sight. Horses meant more to her than humans.

As for John, he made no pretence to be a horseman. He was more at home driving his new Ford Popular (after Marlborough he could never warm to the Ford Prefect). He was Mr Toad setting off from Toad Hall, recklessly toot-tooting along the country lanes to Challow Station where on Mondays, Tuesdays and Wednesdays he took the train to London. He wrote many poems, some of his best wark doncha know, on trains and in railway station waiting rooms. Though he complained loudly and regularly about not having a quiet study of his own he rarely came up with much in a peaceful place. To write he needed the creative juice of frustration. Contentment and comfort was no help to him at all, so being married to The Propellor had on that front been a boon.

In the days just before Christmas 1937, never more than one third awake, muzzy-headed, he often crept out of bed in the early hours to sit with Paul. One night was so bitter he had on his scarf and his hat and some thick socks. The baby cried a lot as John rocked him back to sleep or recited poems to him.

Tarantella worked, the fleas that tease in the High Pyrenees and the wine that tasted of tar. As did *Sea Fever* (one of his father's favourites), all I ask is a tall ship and a star to steer her by, the wheel's kick and the wind's song and the white sail shaking. The recitation was a little ritual in the still of the night, a private thing, just Paul and John and Ernest's silver hip flask, a flask inherited on his death and in regular use, and the lines of verse and the sips of whisky settled John down and they seemed to settle his son down and the poems worked against his private and unspoken fears of losing his son, losing him to meningitis or pneumonia, to influenza or scarlet fever.

He even tried out a couple of his own poems on him, to which (like many a literary critic in the *Observer* or *Times Literary Supplement*) the baby was indifferent.

At the same time, John's head was spinning with all the projects crowding in on him. The price of his success – not that his success ever felt like success – was that he had taken on too much, the Shell Guides to Cornwall and Devon, his next collection of poetry for Jock Murray, his first film for television, not to mention the endless reviewing – but he could handle all this, he could handle anything, he could deal with all those pressures if Paul lived to be a happy boy, or at least a happier boy than he himself had been. No one was ever going to chant *Betjeman's a German spy* to Paul. That was never going to happen to any son of his. As for him being beaten to a pulp with his head under the sink, no, that was a thing of the past. Or just imagine him being put in the basket, no, no, never, never.

John took another sip, if not a slug, from the hip flask.

Paul would not grow up to be a show-off victim at school, or to be a show-off failure at Oxford, or to be an unfaithful husband. He would not make his father's mistakes. He would save his son from all those. Or what on earth was a father for?

But, whatever the pain of the basketing, the past had not been all bad. Indeed, perhaps the pain and the failure was a necessary part of the picture. The American Master had come back into his life, and they were now writing to each other man to man, as if equals, poet to poet. He hadn't seen The American Master since his Highgate Junior School days in the Great War, twenty years or more ago, when out of the blue there was a handwritten letter from him landing on their doormat in freezing Uffington.

The tall, pale-faced young master with horn-rimmed spectacles who rarely smiled was now a tall, pale-faced, middle-aged Director of Faber and Faber with horn-rimmed spectacles who wanted to publish John's next collection of poetry, a tremendous honour, a papal blessing, except that Jock Murray had beaten T.S. Eliot to it.

> Dear Mr Betjeman,
> Yours sincerely,
> T.S. Eliot
> Dear Mr Eliot,
> Yours sincerely,
> John Betjeman
> Dear John, if I may,
> Yours ever,
> Tom Eliot
> Dear and Great Poet,
> Yours gratefully,
> John
> Dear John,
> Dear Uncle Tom,
> Do call on us for a drink at Uffington,
> oh do, if ever you...

As if that wasn't enough of a fillip W.H. Auden had called him a corkingly good comic poet, news he passed on very quietly to his son sleeping in his crib, whispering:

'By the by, little man, guess what, W.H. Auden thinks your father is a corkingly good comic poet. That is what Wystan thinks.'

'What on earth are you doing?'

Penelope, in her long nightdress, was in the doorway. John got clumsily to his feet, almost falling over as he did so. She turned the light on.

'I was just checking,' he said.

'Checking what?'

'Checking that he's all right.'

'Of course he's all right. You're only disturbing him.'

'No, no, I'm not. And I couldn't resist a peep. He may be a tiny tot but he's an absolute winner, isn't he? I feel we're going to get on.'

'Oh, don't talk such self-indulgent guff. That's just your arrested development, which is getting worse by the day. He's ten days old.'

'It's not guff.'

'Stop slobbering and come back to bed, or you'll be grumpier than ever at breakfast.'

'I'm not grumpy at breakfast.'

'Yes, you are. When you turn up.'

'I always turn up.'

'No, you're always looking for your hat or your shoes.'

'Am I? Well, thank you for that.'

'And then you slurp your coffee before running out of the house.'

'Because the house is a shambles, that's why.'

She moved quickly towards her husband, raising a threatening arm.

'Yes, it is a shambles! And instead of spending time with *It* in the middle of the night you might like to spend some time helping *Me* in the middle of the day.'

'What kind of help?'

'Any kind of help. For a start, you could milk the goat.'

'Milk the goat? I hate the fucking goat!'

'Of course you hate the fucking goat, everyone knows that, including the fucking goat. You hate anything that isn't about you.'

'That is ridiculous.'

'I'm absolutely exhausted and you never lift a finger in the kitchen, oh no not you, you never help around the house, you never would help your wife, would you, because it's beneath you, it's too ordinary, you wouldn't want to do anything that obvious, oh no, it's the sort of thing other people do.'

'I do help, I help a lot, I help in lots of different ways.'

'You just write letters to your queer friends and suck up to famous people and keep your famously blinding charm for other women.'

'You just don't see it, do you! I'm getting commissions and writing pieces and doing favours and meeting deadlines to pay the bills and dashing from pillar to post to keep you in bloody horses.'

'And yourself in drink. I can smell the whisky on you even now.'

'You drive me to it.'

'And you're so bloody touchy. But I suppose you think that goes with being creative.'

'Me? Who's being bloody touchy!'

'My father was so so right about you.'

'Oh, the *Field Marshal* was so so right, was he?'

'Yes.'

'Uh-huh. And in what ways was the *Field Marshal* so so right?'

'Just go back to bed, back to Archie,' she hissed.

'I will, don't worry. I'm off.'

'Perhaps he can help you with your persecution mania.'

He pushed past her, raging.

'God, you can be unpleasant!'

'It's called straight talking.'

'You really know how to hit below the belt, don't you?'

Paul was now crying. She shouted,

'Now look what you've done!'

'What *I've* done!'

'Yes. Shut up, shut up, *shut up!*'

Their German *au pair* thought Shut Up was John's Christian name, she heard it so often.

38 | A CHILD ILL

Oh, little body, do not die.
The soul looks out through wide blue eyes
So questioningly into mine,
That my tormented soul replies:

"Oh, little body, do not die.
You hold the soul that talks to me
Although our conversation be
As wordless as the windy sky."

So looked my father at the last
 Right in my soul, before he died,
Though words we spoke went heedless past
As London traffic-roar outside.

And now the same blue eyes I see
 Look through me from a little son,
So questioning, so searchingly
That youthfulness and age are one.

My father looked at me and died
 Before my soul made full reply.
Lord, leave this other Light alight —
 Oh, little body, do not die.

A s I was about to walk along to the Warwick Road underground at the end of a long day in the studio I caught
sight of Ben Whitrow. He was stooping down into a taxi,
obviously keen to be on his way home to Wimbledon. When
you're getting on a bit it often shows, as I am finding, when
you are stepping in and out of a car. And, whatever age you
are, these long days in the studio do take it out of you: the
concentration, the demand for perfection, the company of
younger talented colleagues, the way you have to be 'up' for
each take, relaxed but sharp, tolerant but tough. I wanted to
say well done to Ben but that could wait till the morrow and,
anyway, you have to be careful, always careful, never to sound
bland or pat. There would be other chances for a private word.

And the chance came. At our lunch break on the third day
he was standing in reception with the other actors when he
saw me. He nodded and called over his shoulder to the others,

'Bye, everyone, I'm off to suck up to the writer.'

And we were out, just the two of us, out into the streets
of Maida Vale.

'Where are we going?'

'There's a place in the park,' I said, 'ten minutes walk.'

'I can manage that.'

'We can get a bite there.'

He held up a plastic carrier bag.

'Do you think they'll mind if I eat my own?'

'If it gets nasty I'll defend you.'

At the café I had today's soup is carrot and a hot bread roll,
conservative as ever, and Ben sat in the corner and unwrapped
his smoked salmon sandwich in a mock furtive manner. I
could see he also had a hard-boiled egg, one of those things
difficult to peel in a neat way. You always end up with a small
bit of shell either stuck on your tongue or lips or on your

fingers or all the above.

He made a little naughty boy play of hiding his sandwich when a man brought me my soup.

'Did you know my father was a teacher, Jonathan?'

'No, I didn't. So was mine.'

'He taught History. And he always said of teachers, if you're going to survive in the classroom there has to be a bit of you somewhere, some-where, that your pupils fear. A bit of you that, if provoked, could turn.'

'I think that's right.'

'And that's in you?'

'Yes,' I said.

'But well hidden?'

'I hope so. But if it's open conflict, if it gets down to them or you, it's got to be you.'

Ben perked up.

'So, Jonathan, if I'm arsing around in *your* class at Tonbridge what do you do? If I'm being a real pain, which I could be, a real little smart arse, answering back, how do you handle me?'

'I'm not sure.'

His eyes challenged me.

'Yes you are. What would you do?'

And I don't know why I did this, as it's not my kind of thing, but perhaps I had subconsciously remembered Ben's 1985 performance in our sitting room. I put down my soup spoon and stood up and walked slowly and casually round the table and stood just behind Ben's back, and I stayed there until he stopped eating his sandwich and I could feel him stirring and getting uncomfortable. Then, not making a sound, I leant forward and whispered very quietly and privately in his ear, 'If I were you, Whitrow, I wouldn't do that again. And don't think I can't see you eating.'

Then I straightened up and walked back to my seat. Ben was beaming.

'Awfully good, that.'

'Thank you.'

'Ever think about acting, you know, about doing it? Professionally.'

'No, never. Mind you, schoolteachers are variety artistes. Sort of.'

'I suppose you are.'

'But I acted a bit at school, as a boy, and loved it. Shakespeare.'

'Who did you play?'

'Cleomenes.'

'Cleomenes?'

'In *The Winter's Tale.*'

Ben frowned.

'Cleomenes? I've been in *The Winter's Tale*. I played Camillo. And there's no Cleomenes.'

He started to unpeel his hard-boiled egg.

'Well,' I said, 'there is a Cleomenes. He's a minor lord. Very minor. Blink and you missed me. But you were far too grand to notice. I can do Cleomenes for you now, if you like. *The climate's delicate, the air most sweet*... the next year, this would be 1958, there was a new producer of the school play, and I was cast as Sir Andrew Aguecheek.'

'Ooo, now we're talking. Sir Andrew! What a part!'

'The tallest man in Illyria.'

'*I was adored once too!*'

I was at boarding school in Wales, in Brecon, a town not so many miles from where *Under Milk Wood* is set, and fewer miles still from Bruce Chatwin's *On the Black Hill*. And *Twelfth Night* was the 1958 school play. There was one dramatic production a year, just the one, only the one. The school play. The School Play. The choice seemed to boil down to Shakespeare or Gilbert and Sullivan.

This was in the days before Drama was considered a serious subject at school, before it was a worthwhile subject with lessons and exams and a proper place of its own in the timetable. This was in the days when dressing up and pretending to be another person was considered a rather dodgy, if not harmful, activity. Anyone interested in the arts was considered morally shaky. To say that Drama was mistrusted in my schooldays is to put it far too lightly. After all, hadn't Plato taken a dim view of imitation?

Anyway, I was cast – *typecast*, one friend unkindly suggested – as Sir Andrew Aguecheek, the long-haired fop, Sir Andrew Agueface, as tall as any man in Illyria, a witless wet, a fool and a prodigal, an absurdly effeminate would-be wooer, and the butt of every sexual joke that Sir Toby Belch could let fly.

I loved being Sir Andrew Aguecheek as much as Ben Whitrow enjoyed being Sir John Betjeman.

In Act One, Scenes One and Two, I waited off stage, waited in the wings with my heart hammering, waited while the boring main plot stuff was established before they made way for the fun and games, i.e. for me and the lads to come on and cry havoc. In Scene Three I sidled on stage, as thin as a lamp-post, wearing a long blonde wig:

Sir Andrew: *How now, Sir Toby Belch.*
Sir Toby: *Sweet Sir Andrew.*

Sir Andrew: *Bless you, fair shrew.*
Maria: *And you too, sir.*

Even writing down those words transports me (as did hearing them again years later in the all-male Mark Rylance production at the Globe Theatre). My 1950s schooldays consisted mostly of Classics and chapel, rugby and prayers, cricket and Cicero, but here, just the once, once a year, for three nights only, there was Drama and the chance to be someone else and more myself. Oh, *give me excess of it*: a comedy written in 1601 had, after a fashion, liberated me. Or at least started the long process, one I'm still on.

As was the custom then in single-sex boarding schools – and I'm told still is so at Harrow – the girls' parts were taken by boys. Boys were all there were. Dear God, it's coming back to me, as if it were yesterday, from aged ten to eighteen, eight years of it. In the dormitories the only distinguishing feature between the red-blanketed mattresses, which were lined up three feet apart, was the colour of the rugs (neatly folded) which we were allowed to keep at the foot of the bed. Not a teddy bear in sight.

I was in Kids Dorm (for two years), Bathroom Dorm (two years), Barn Dorm (two years) and Top Dorm (two years). On a quick tot-up I make that approximately two thousand dormitory nights. Until I got to Cambridge, where I shared a set of rooms with one man, that is how it was. Sixty years later, returning to my old school to give a talk to the staff, I found I could still walk round my boarding house with my eyes closed and not miss a step on the staircase or the landings, let alone bump into a door frame, though some of the light switches had changed their position.

There was one other change. It is now a girls' house.

In all honesty, a bit too late for me.

Still, in the 1950s it was, as I said, all boys. All boys was normal, so to speak. So, when it came to auditioning and then casting *Twelfth Night*, the captivating Viola was a scrum half, Olivia, the haughty countess, was a back row forward, while Maria, the waiting gentlewoman (the part the young John Betjeman had played in Marlborough in the 1920s) was a hooker who looked more at home in the front of the line-out than he did in a maid's dress.

Twelfth Night is, of course, all about love, and for much of the play and for most of the characters that love is unrequited. Viola loves Orsino, Orsino loves Olivia, Olivia loves Viola/ Cesario, Malvolio loves Olivia, Sir Andrew loves... and so on. As you will remember – a teacher's stock line which means you won't remember, if you ever knew, and what's more you don't care, so I'll spell it out one more time – as you will remember, the plot of *Twelfth Night* demands that Viola, in her role as a go-between, must disguise herself as the boy/youth Cesario. So, just to be clear, a rugby-playing boy actor is given the part of a girl (Viola) who then has to dress up as a boy (Cesario), which is not all that demanding given that the actor playing Viola is a boy already.

Mind you, it isn't all that easy either, because the boy actor who is playing the part of the girl Viola and who then has to go around in disguise as the boy Cesario is required to display a comic 'male' swagger to suggest that he is a young wench in a boy's clothes who hasn't quite conquered male walking, whereas, as I've just explained, he is really a chunky scrum half who in real life trudges from line-out to line-out like the boy rugby player he is.

Shakespeare followed similar plot paths in both *As You Like It* and *The Merchant of Venice*. In the Forest of Arden the female Rosalind becomes the male Ganymede ('I swear I am not that I play'), while in *The Merchant of Venice* Portia appears as the male Doctor of Law, turning mincing steps into manly strides as she/he travels from Belmont to Venice to carry out a crucial role in the trial and humiliation of Shylock, a part played at school by Ben Whitrow.

In considering all this, it is not my instinct that Shakespeare was suffering from any gender category crisis. Yes, he had a foot in both camps, if not a camp foot in both worlds, and it allowed him a chance to play bo-peep, to get away with things in an undercover way. But he was also an actor-playwright having fun, and that was how it always felt in rehearsals when Viola, Olivia, Maria and I came straight from the sports fields, with no time for a communal bath, took our rugby boots off at the door to the gym (which doubled as our theatre), climbed up on to the bare boards of the stage and left wet footprints with our squelching socks.

What is love? 'Tis not hereafter:
Present mirth hath present laughter.
What's to come is still unsure.
In delay there lies no plenty,
Then come kiss me sweet and twenty,
Youth's a stuff will not endure.

On that stage we rehearsed in front of a badly painted pastoral backcloth and under the most minimal lighting (up a ladder the master i/c lighting would call down to the director, 'So, do you want them on or off?'). No matter, I was happy, with that happiness that gives you a surge in your veins. As a boy in a sports-mad school I was used to being in front of a crowd, clattering down the pavilion steps in my studs and crossing the white line on to a cricket or rugby pitch, but this was different. It was much more than just the three performance nights, more than putting Factor 5 or Factor 9 on to our spotty faces or watching others fitting on their falsies and applying beauty spots, more than opening up the big tubs of make-up remover and plunging our fingers into the goey stuff: the thing was, I felt alive as I never had before.

In dressing up, and in cross-dressing, it is possible we expose more of ourselves than we do in our everyday lives. At the time I never talked about all this to anyone, and never have since, but while rehearsing and overcoming my fears about performing on a stage I read new looks on the faces of my school-friends and, though not at that age particularly given to self-analysis, I glimpsed sides of myself I had not sensed before.

In his poem *The Play Way*, Seamus Heaney describes creative writing in a classroom. The teacher, presumably Heaney himself, puts a record on the gramophone to see what, if anything, the music might unlock and let loose in his pupils. The strategy and the music works. With the blundering embrace of the free word the young are snared, as *They trip / To fall into themselves unknowingly*.

Acting in school plays helped me to fall into myself. As it helped Ben Whitrow. And the more Ben and I swapped stories the more we found in common not only with each other but also with Betjeman.

41 | THE CHURCH IN THE SAND, 1948

There are treble voices on the wind. Along the sands timeless beach cricket is being played, between fathers and sons, with that moving boundary line, the sea, the sea. This is Daymer Bay. This is North Cornwall. A bat hits a soft ball high in the air and a boy, a bare-footed boy of about ten, sets off on his scampering run between the wickets. A bespectacled man in a black one-piece bathing costume, mouth open, eyes staring into the sun, is circling under the descending ball. Those on the beach who know anything at all about cricket do not expect him to catch it. The signs are not promising.

Indeed they think he might not even lay a finger on it.

'*Mine*!' the man shouts. 'And... you're out, Paul. You're out.'

'But you dropped it!'

'No, I didn't.'

'You did! I saw you. It went right through your hands.'

'You're out, chum.'

'I'm not.'

'I'm batting now and you're bowling.'

'You dropped it, Daddy! You're a beastly swizz.'

'Hand over the bat, give it here, it's my turn. *Prawn*!'

'But I'm still in.'

'Paul.'

'And you can't catch. You always drop it.'

'No, I don't'

'Mummy catches better than you.'

'Good, well, go and play with her then. Go and play with The Bulldozer. And take the stumps with you. What a relief! I'll go to the rock pools with Wibz.'

'And you can't ride a horse. You're hopeless on a horse.'

'I don't want to ride a horse. I hate horses.'

'I'm going to tell Mummy you said that!'

★

A few years later, they sat on the headland above the same Daymer Bay, the same restless father and the same uncomfortable son. They sat side by side. While his father was talking about the church, Paul's eyes were scanning the golf course, seeing if there were any players coming down the fairway. There weren't.

'Over the years St Enodoc has been known by various names. In fact quite a few.'

The restless father waited for a response from the uncom-

163

fortable son. There was none.

'Because I admit that I collect church history rather in the way your mother collects goats.'

'Does she collect goats? She's got one.'

'Do try not to be so literal And, here's another thing, did you know, and this might amuse you, the devil, or so they believed in medieval times, always lived on the north side of a church, which is why you'll find more people buried on the south. Including your grandmother. Paul?'

'I'm listening, Father.'

'The very first reference to this church was way back in 1299. And it's been known as St Guinedocus, and at another stage it was Sanctus Wenodocus, as well as Sinking Nedy or Sinkinny. Sinkinny, of course, was because... yes? yes? because It... Was... Sink-ing, not too difficult to work out, because the church was completely... '

'Father, I don't want – I don't want to go back, to go back to – '

'The doorway is fourteenth century... The vestry is... Norman. Clearly Norman, as any fool can see. The transept is... what? You don't want to what?'

'To go back to school.'

'Yes, you do. Did I really never tell you, dear boy, that St Enodoc Church was once covered completely in sand?'

'No, Father,' he lied.

'Oh, yes, it went right up to the eaves. Can you imagine it? It sounds like a tall story or a fairy tale. But that's how it was for a number of decades from the beginning to the middle of the nineteenth century. Rather as the Anglican church was nearly buried by doubts and discords and dissension. Anyway, you could only see the steeple sticking up, and the poor old clergyman could only get in by being lowered down through a skylight. That must have been a sight to behold.'

'So there were no services on Sundays?'

'None of any kind at all. The place, as I said, was buried in sand. Nature had taken over, like nettles and cow parsley take over a narrow path in late May. Or Queen Anne's lace. But didn't I give you *In the Roar of the Sea* to read? I thought I did. Some while ago now?'

'Did you?'

'By Sabine Baring-Gould. You remember, the novelist and hymn writer, yes you do, he wrote *Now the Day is Over* and *Onward Christian Soldiers*? And many other hymns. I'm sure I gave the novel to you.'

'Oh, yes, you did.'

'But you haven't read it, little man, have you?'

'I was going to but Candida took it.'

'Well, Wibbly-Wobbly does read books. She is what I would call a reader. She takes after me. You are not a reader, and it is high time you were, a point made yet again on your end of term report. And you'd like that book, *In the Roar of the Sea*, any boy would, it's just about the first adult book I ever read, albeit second division Stevenson. It's a ripping yarn about smugglers and shipwrecks on this coast, with the sea licking its chops. The story starts right there, in that very churchyard.'

'Were you lonely down here, father?'

'What?'

'Were you left on your own a lot? When you were young?'

'Down here?'

'In Cornwall, when you were a boy, with grandpa and grandma?'

'Lonely? Gosh, no! Each year, each hols, there were lots of young ones, hearty boys and jolly girls, there was Ralph and then there was Biddy and others, can't remember who, they'll come back to me in a minute, usually the children of beaks. And in no time at all, in the way you do, we became a gang of chums who met up on the beach. We made sandcastles with turrets and moats and we had treasure hunts and we whistled, whistling was very important, you had to be able to whistle, and we bicycled around the lanes with our hands in our pockets. And I can still hear that special sound of the tennis ball on a racket, and of course tennis brought out the gels, and I could see that they weren't like boys.'

'What is a queer?'

'I have to say these questions of yours are coming a bit thick and fast today. Why do you ask? Any special reason?'

The boy blew his fringe out of his eyes.

'Mother says that your friends are queers.'

'Some are, some are.'

'Do they have girl friends as well?'

'The point is, the point is that they are my friends, that's what matters. Going back to the church and the sand, the vicar raised the money, and since you keep on about it, he may have been a queer for all I know or care, perhaps they all are, the point was he believed in God and he led his flock and he raised a great sum of money, this was back in the 1860s, to return the church to its former glory. He led a team of local workmen, doing everything himself that he asked them to do, and they came over the dunes and down Daymer Lane in all weathers, in their hours off work, all with their spades and shovels and carts, and they cleared it, the whole jolly lot, and you know how heavy sand is, it took them months, took them years of backbreaking labour, and they restored it to a place of worship. To this church before our eyes. Isn't that wonderful? Can you imagine what it felt to them, as the church slowly reappeared under their hands? How revealing in every sense! Don't you agree?'

'Yes.'

'That sense of rediscovery, seeing a bit more every season, uncovering the past to guide you in the present, scraping and digging down, often with their bare fingers. Because they loved their church. To them the church was central, essential, the true heart of the place. I repeat, isn't that rather wonderful? A real labour of love. If only the Church of England had more parishioners like them now. Paul?'

'Did they go on playing golf?'

'What?'

'Golf. When the church was covered in sand? The golfers.'

'Oh, there was no golf course then, you simpleton! There were no golf courses in the middle of the nineteenth century.'

'There were. They played golf in Fife in the fifteenth century.'

'Did they?'

'Fife is on the east coast of Scotland.'

'Yes yes, I know perfectly well where Fife is, but I didn't know about the golf in the fifteenth century.'

'They hit a pebble with a stick around the dunes. Sometimes the pebbles got lost down rabbit runs.'

'Did they!'

'By the seventeenth century it was quite a popular game. Then they started to call their sticks clubs.'

'What an amazing boy you are. A thousand apologies if I appeared rude. Whatever next!'

'Why do you and mother shout at each other so much?'

'Do we?'

'Yes, all the time.'

'Sometimes, perhaps, not all the time, but then all married couples have occasional ding-dongs.'

'It's not nice waking up hearing you.'

'No, I'm sure it's not.'

'It happens most days. Even on holiday. I'm frightened to come downstairs.'

'I'm sure it's not nice. Put like that, it's a bit... numbing. And humbling.'

'I shouldn't have said it. I'm sorry.'

'No, no, I am. I am. I'm the one who should be sorry. And

I do love you.'

'I love you too, Daddy.'

John started to tap his pockets. Then he rummaged.

'I shouldn't really be doing this, not here,' he said, pointing to the cigarette he was lighting up. 'And here,' he rummaged again, 'take this, take it', he said, slipping him half a crown. 'That should bolster your bank balance a bit. And here's another one.'

'Thank you.'

The boy held on tightly to the warm coins and sniffed them. They smelt of cigarette smoke. The boy pushed his fringe away from his forehead and put the half crowns in his pocket.

His father stood up.

'Right, off I go to meet another deadline. Another article, another bit of flotsam. I'm nothing more than a hack, I realise that, and please do not ask me what a hack is.'

'I won't.'

'No wonder I never write any new poems.'

They made their way along the beach.

'What will you be writing about this time, Daddy?'

'Books. Not your neck of the woods.'

42 | PENELOPE CROSSES OVER, 1948

It was, he sometimes said to his closest friends, the worst day of his life. The marriage had been bad for years. How bad? Well, since you ask it was embarrassingly bad, what with their bawling falling on deaf ears, chasing each other in and out of the bathroom, screaming, throwing shoes, running downstairs and out of the front door into the garden, alarming the horses, alarming the goat(s), John jumping wild-eyed on a train for London or Cornwall, then both of them trying from an enforced distance to lay off each other and trying to patch things up by letter until letters felt the only way left, the written word their final refuge. The post had become their communion.

She had long found little to amuse her in sex. When she and John were far apart they were fine. Indeed, everything between them could appear more or less happy, until they met up again in the flesh.

One morning, a damp still day on the Berkshire downs, Penelope sought him out in his study and closed the door firmly behind her. He did not look up.

'John.'

'What is it?'

'I need to talk to you.'

'I'm in the middle of something.'

'I can see that.'

'It'll have to wait.'

'It can't. Because I know what I'm going to say will hurt you. I really do.'

'Ah.'

'But try not to get into a flap.'

He gave a little laugh, screwed up the piece he was writing into a little ball and threw it at the waste paper basket, and missed by a fair margin.

'Oh, you're going to hurt me a little bit more, are you?'

'But you must understand why I had to do it.'

He swung round.

'Do what?'

'I'm about to explain.'

'It's not about the children, is it? What are you up to? It's not about Paul or Candida?'

'I am converting.'

'What?'

'I'm converting.'

'To Rome?'

'Yes.'

'No. No, you're not.'

'I am.'

'You wouldn't.'

She opened her hands.

'And I feel, I do feel that I have at last come home.'

'Home! Is that the word you just used? Did you say *home*?'

'Yes.'

'Well, it's a different home from mine.'

He stood up.

'Yes, I know that, but I do want you to come with me. I think you should. And I think, in time, you will.'

'Have you gone barmy?'

'No.'

'Then what's happened?'

'If we're talking barmy, if anyone in this house is off his rocker, John, it's you.'

'Me?'

'You're chockful of phobias.'

'What's wrong with you today? Sit down.'

'I don't want to sit down. And there's nothing wrong with me. All I'm trying to do is make you see something very straightforward. I. Am. Converting.'

He put his head in his hands.

'Why is our Church, something you can always turn to, suddenly not good enough for you?'

'It's far from sudden, I can assure you.'

'We've just seen off the bloody Nazis and you want me to ditch the church I love and always have loved and swear allegiance to –'

'No, not to –'

His voice leapt a register.

'To a Church whose pope sat on the bloody fence in the war and made a *concordat* with Mussolini!'

'Not to a Pope, to the truth. The truth.'

'Is the Pope's truth any different from the Archbishop's? We say the same creed, we read the same Bible, although ours has better English. Or does Latin make all the difference?'

'I want a Church with authority.'

'Authority! Oh, we like authority now, do we?'

She stuck out her chin.

'Not a church which provides for all tastes.'

'Spare me that old chestnut. Our Church, my Church, has many rooms. You don't have to be a religious maniac and live in fear of hell-fire.'

'That's not good enough for me, John, and it ought not to be good enough for you.'

'Damn it all, Penelope, we left Rome because the papacy stank, and the Church of England has gone on teaching Christ's message with great devotion and beauty.'

'The Church of England does not have the Mass at its heart. The Church of England is not the real thing.'

Before she could finish the phrase he smacked the table.

'Not the real thing?'

'Not the real thing.'

'For me it is.'

'You want doubts, John, you enjoy them, and I don't. Doubts are probably good for your poetry.'

'Keep my poetry out of this! You don't know the first bloody thing about poetry. Stick to ponies.'

'Oh, I will stick to ponies, don't you worry. Listen, no, just for one moment in your life, listen. There are millions of Anglicans who would see your high church ways as popish. They can't see the difference.'

'They are quite different and you –'

'I have only one life on this earth and I cannot go on resisting the truth of the Catholic church.'

'So, that's it? That's it? The parting of the ways?'

'Yes.'

'We will never take communion again together? Never go to boring parish church council meetings together? Never produce the Nativity play? This is ridiculous. You're an Anglican through and through, you're always quarrelling with the vicar.'

'No, don't try your jokes. Keep your charm and your yap yap for your other women.'

'The church is our bond! Our deepest bond. The Church of England! I mean I thought you might be toying with the idea but I didn't think you were serious.'

'I don't toy. I'm totally serious. How can this be a shock to you? Haven't you seen it coming?'

'Of course I haven't! You're deserting me.'

'Don't you dare talk to me about deserting. Not with your record.'

'That's what it is. Desertion.'

'I've made up my mind. I've been taking instruction. For a long time now.'

'Instruction from whom? How come I didn't know about this!'

'Because you're always catching a train. If I'm the bossy one it's because you're always absent, you're never here, you're with someone else or with your latest, you're anywhere but here, and when you're here you're not here.'

'Oh, I know who's behind this.'

'Who?'

'Evelyn Ghastly Waugh.'

'Wrong.'

'Arthur Evelyn St John Waugh, the famous Catholic convert. He tried every tactic to bully me into converting, tried for months and failed, so he's moved on to you!'

'No, it's entirely my decision.'

'Not content with stealing my teddy bear for his bloody Brideshead novel he had the cheek to dedicate a book to you, and that's turned your head –'

'Evelyn had nothing whatsoever to do with it.'

They glared at each other and took stock before she continued in a quieter voice,

'If you want to know I had a vision.'

'A vision?'

'Of the heavenly host.'

'You what? When was this?'

'Last year.'

'Where?'

'In Assissi.'

'I knew nothing good would come out of that trip.'

'That's not funny, John. Not in the slightest. But typical.'

And go she did. In St Aloysius Church in Oxford. On the 9th of March 1948. Paul was ten. Candida was six. John could not bear the whole business so he went down on his own to Cornwall. In fact he walked across the golf course to his seat in St Enodoc and he was sitting there in the churchyard while she went over, as they say, to Rome.

And that was it. It was all over. Everything.

43 | ENOUGH IS ENOUGH

He had always talked to himself a lot, in good times and in bad, and he often asked himself the same question, and the question was… is there a day…

Is there a day when you look at your wife, or your wife looks at you, and you think I can't go on with this, I really can't? The phrase keeps repeating itself. It can't go on, can it, I can't go on, he, she or it can't go on, we, you, they can't go on. But it did go on. Go on it did.

Is there, though, an episode, a moment, when you finally

recognise that nothing will be the same again and you can no longer ignore the truth? The truth that you have drifted irretrievably apart. That you are wincing or tuning out when they speak. That they're a bad earache. That where once there was love now there is not.

Is there a day when you decide that tolerance has its limits? That even if you share a bed, the sex side has its limits. There may still be love of a sort but, given this latest episode, given this latest decision, you would rather not be left together in the same bed or the same room or eat at the same table or have to sit side by side in the front of the same vehicle. That you are looking forward to the moment when she or you, it really does not matter which, walks alone out of the front door, and escapes. Because you just want the distance between you, you don't want to have to listen any more, and once you have walked out and got that distance between you, Phew!

He talked to himself a lot.

Yes, he had seen it coming.

What words did he use?

Yes, I had seen it coming. Because I am not a fool. But I pretended to myself that it could never happen, not the full force of it. As I said, I am not a fool, or not a complete fool, but I do have the capacity to go on fooling myself for years, looking only half of my life in the face, or less, or looking away when the music stops. In some ways I am always writing a script in which not only am I the central player but everyone else is complicit in my court jester role. And that court jester performance blinds me to myself as well as others to me.

How does it work?

I have talked at length to you about this matter, Lord, but to be perfectly honest I have come to doubt that I am holding your interest. You must surely have more riveting material to hand. So I have decided to give You a breather and I have recently tried hard, tried very hard, to confront this in a sensible everyday way and I think it best to describe it objectively.

I walk into the room and smile and perform and cackle and flirt and tease and regale them with anecdotes and laugh at some pompous old trout's joke and in this way I make them all feel good about themselves, I make them all feel warm and witty, even make wonderfully boring people feel warm and witty and in no time at all they feel warm and wonderful about me.

It's a game and it plays out (mostly) to my credit. I have a gift for telling stories in which I make up not only the lines that I say I said but also the lines I say that the other person said, which they didn't, and so fiction becomes fact. Then, if not well before then, I drink too much and get merry, and this helps me to believe that I did really say those things and so did my fellow actors or co-conspirators.

So absolutely everyone is a winner. No wonder I am into the blarney and on every chat show on the telly. No wonder I go down well in Dublin and Donegal, in Cork and Connemara.

The Propellor has no truck with any such stuff. In fact she had no truck with me from the very start. She says my manner is a garden party of guff and gush. You only have to hear the ways she says the words *guff* and *gush* to find yourself sobering up. And this deflation tends to send me into a downward spiral of self-pity and self-indulgence, and takes a toll on my temper. With our tempers now lost, she says that I am off my rocker, and when The Propellor writes that statement in one of her long letters she uses capitals. In the middle of a paragraph you come across YOU ARE OFF YOUR ROCKER. Although I now give her letters only the quickest of scans, it's still hard for those banner headlines not to catch your half-averted eye. You can't really miss it, can you? It caught your eye just now, I bet.

She is a realist who boxes me into a corner. She dances around me like that chap Cassius Clay, jabbing, jabbing. Left

175

hand jabs to the head and then one to the heart. She says I neglect the truth, jab jab, that I am a show-off who enjoys guilt, jab jab, that I spend all our money on myself, and that I make things up. She says that people who make things up are LIARS. (She does love that word, especially in capitals.)

Well, I am a writer. Writers tell stories, don't they? Writers make things up. But it's not as clear cut as that. We make things up on one level and on another level we don't make things up. Inside it's all together, all part and parcel of a made-up truth.

There is no way, though, that I can pretty up the fact that after 9th March 1948 our paths parted. I am making nothing up when I say with no hint of a lie that it was a body blow. When I was forty-two, when Penelope was thirty-eight, when The Powlie was ten and Wibbly-Wobbly six, Penelope crossed the road, and went over to Rome, or was (if you prefer the other angle) received into the Roman Catholic Church, which she calls the one true church, which always strikes me as a bit rich not to say appallingly arrogant. Or she defected from the Church of England to Rome. Dress it in any language you will, put it any way you like, it is what she would call A FACT.

As a final twist of the knife, the defection took place in my beloved Oxford, in her beloved St Aloysius Church, Oxford – or the Oxford Oratory – in the Woodstock Road. I was not there to witness it. Father Michael and Father Rupert were there to see her clasped to the bosom of the one true church, as no doubt were Brothers Tom, Dick and Harry.

With the children farmed out (or palmed off, if you are feeling critical of their father) I went on my own on the nine o'clock down to Cornwall. My favourite train journey to my favourite place had never seemed so long, Bodmin never bleaker, nor the landscape more flat. Our house in Daymer Lane, if you could still call it 'ours', felt damp and was damp. Of course there was no food to eat and no fire in the grate and no Archie in bed so I drank whisky and water steadily at the kitchen table and slept fitfully on my own.

Waking to a grey, mizzly, headachy day – a March morning and a March afternoon I somehow had to kill – I put on my mackintosh and was soon past St Enodoc, with barely a glance at the church, and then set off across the overcast golf course. I had to walk. To numb the pain and to pass the time I had to walk, had to keep walking. I sometimes pass people with that look, that self-absorbed had-to-walk look.

Dropping down to Rock I had the ferry to Padstow all to myself (there were no holiday makers waiting on the slipway, no young families lining up on the sand). Leaning against the Padstow harbour wall I ate a Cornish pasty of lamb gristle and hard potato, and it has to be a pasty as bad as that to make a hangover worse, and I bought a newspaper and walked aimlessly round the town and on up to the war memorial and sat on one of the benches and looked back over the water to Rock and the golf course and watched a limp sail or two going slowly in or out of Padstow.

I tried to read the paper, with spots of rain hitting the newsprint, but I could not concentrate. I checked my watch. In less than another hour she would be doing it. Going over to Rome, being received, lost for ever. It was trying to rain, so I turned round and went back down to the harbour and came back across the estuary, raising the eyebrow of the grumpy ferryman.

'Not much to keep you?' he said.

I shrugged and shook my head.

'No, not today, sadly.'

I was not going potty. And I would not go potty. We are often tougher than we think. If I had survived Evelyn Waugh's hateful bullying on behalf of his version of Rome, and there would be more in the pipeline from him, I could survive this. In a minute or two I would go inside the church and shelter from the storm. The rain had now set in, set in so low I could barely see beyond Brae Hill let alone make out the horizon on the Atlantic.

The backs of my trousers were clinging to my calves. Right, I am an Anglican, she is a Roman Catholic, there's nothing good about The Propellor's decision, this is horrible, but I can't change it and I will go on my own into the church, socks squelching, and sit and pray. Might as well get on with the new dispensation. Life will go on, as it does, what can you do, you have to get on with it, don't you, but it will never be the same.

When Robert Louis Stevenson stopped going to church with his father, his father stopped whistling. And he never whistled again.

44 | GETTING INTO BETJEMAN

As we walked slowly round and out of Paddington Park, past the pole vaulter, past the young mothers with their baby buggies, and past the dustbins, Ben told me about his long depression. I did not know how bad, how deep, it had been. How he woke up each morning thinking oh, no, not another bloody day. How only the thought of being Betjeman had kept him going, how the prospect of being Betjeman had got him out of bed in the morning and stopped him getting straight back in. How he relished being him.

And, hearing this, I heard myself telling Ben about my own problems, my condition, which up till then I had kept hidden. If you're an actor or a writer you don't want people to know such personal things because you might never be asked to work again. You could all too easily be written off.

After that we walked on for a while without speaking, allowing it to sink in. Was he walking slowly for me or was I walking slowly for him?

'When did you first get into Betjeman, Ben?'

'I can't remember when I wasn't.'

'Really?'

'In a serious way, you mean?'

'Whatever.'

'Probably when I read The Arrest of Oscar Wilde at the Cadogan Hotel. I used to be able to do it, by heart, the whole poem.'

'Go on then.'

'Used to, I said. Can't now. It's gone. A lot's gone, sad to say, including the girls, and I do miss that.'

'You're sounding like Betj more and more. Not enough sex.'

'He had such a flirty touch, didn't he?'

'Betj the Letch.'

'Ending those letters of his with "Thinking of your curves".'

'And, what was the other one, "You attract me physically as well as spiritually." Such a good line.'

'What about "Your sulky lips"?'

'And "When can I zip up your dress?" '

We stopped on the pavement to laugh. As we slowly sauntered on, Ben said:

'He loved women, had pashes all the time. Penelope and Elizabeth lasted, in their very different ways, Feeble was the love of his life, no doubt at all, but there was always another girl on the go. Those were the days.'

'I think he appealed to their protective instincts.'

'Interesting, tell me more,' Ben said.

'Well, he was always looking for reassurance, for consolation. Some men play on that. He didn't mind being vulnerable in public, and with a certain kind of girl that goes down very well.'

'Not with Penelope.'

'Not with Penelope, no.'

'It drove her nuts. And he was never around to help. Bit of a hopeless father.'

'Hang on,' I said, 'Candida adored him.'

'True, but for him the baby was always yelling.'

'Well, they do, babies, don't they?'

Then Ben calmly announced, 'I was at the same prep school as Betj, you know.'

'The Dragon in Oxford!'

'Yes. Didn't you know?'

'No, I did not know.'

'Where we were encouraged to be pert.'

'All these connections with Betjeman, I can't believe it, Ben, and now you tell me. After I've written the plays.'

'And I was a boy there with Paul, his son. At the Dragon.'

'You knew Paul as well?'

'Sorry, thought I'd told you, we were more or less contemporaries. Belly-flopped into the river together.'

'I give up!'

I'm not sure if I was exasperated or pretending to be. That is often my way with friends.

'Betj came to give us a poetry reading. I didn't know Paul well. I'd like to have done. To begin with he was the apple of his father's eye. His firstborn, his son.'

'So, what went wrong? I can see it with Ernie and John, trade v snobbery and all that, but why John and Paul?'

'God knows.' Ben looked away. We walked on.

His voice was very soft. He went on,

'So much remains private in life, half-hidden, doesn't it? We only know half the story, at best.'

'Because we live part of our lives in secret?'

'Quite a big part, I'd say. You tell me, why do things go wrong with people in their private lives, even people we think we know very well? Quite often, nobody knows.'

'Ah, the Paul Brady song. Nobody knows why Elvis threw it all away. Nobody knows what Ruby had to hide. Nobody knows why some of us have broken hearts...'

'I don't know Paul Brady. Should I?'

'An Irish singer-songwriter,' I said. 'Very good.'

Ben's eyes ran round the street, his face hangdog sad. Then he said,

'Just a thought. About Paul. A hunch. May be wrong.'

'Yes?'

'Fathers and sons, it's a thing about successful fathers and sons.'

'Yes?'

'Perhaps Betj didn't take Paul seriously. You have to take your children seriously. Not all the time of course, that's unrealistic, that's bollocks. The thing is, we all need to be loved, that's a given, but we all need to be rated too. Taken seriously.'

'Totally agree,' I said. 'Teaching taught me that.'

'And at 80 I still do,' he said, 'Even at this age, I still want to be rated.'

'Don't worry, you are.'

'But I think nicknames may have had something to do with it.'

'Nicknames. Yes.'

'I think Paul felt they were laughing at him as he grew up. And they were, dammit. I mean, being called those names, what does that do to you? The Prawn. The Egg. The Powlie. I'm glad it wasn't me on the receiving end. I'd have lashed out. But for some reason they thought it was funny.'

'And Penelope joined in. Unusual for a mother to do that, isn't it? Mind you, she was an unusual mother.'

'Anything for a laugh, wasn't that it, wasn't that the Betjeman way? The Betjeman habit?'

'Even so,' I said.

'You could end up feeling a freak. So eventually Paul ran

away. Later, in his twenties. As far as he could. I don't blame him.'

'It's a posh thing,' I said.

Ben stopped.

'What is?'

'All these nicknames, Feeble for Elizabeth, The Propellor for Penelope, and so on. These baby-talk nicknames.'

'They're quite fun,' Ben said.

'No, they're not,' I said, 'they're bloody silly. Isn't it an upper-class preserve, isn't it their version of arrested development? Because they seem to specialise in it. And Betjeman wanted so much to be part of that class, that set, didn't he? He wanted to be in, he craved acceptance in the big houses.'

'Well, he was full of fear, wasn't he, so insecure, poor chap, and yet got on wonderfully well with Candida,' Ben said, waving it all away with his hand, suddenly tiring of the topic. He nodded slightly in the direction of the BBC studios which we were approaching. 'How do you think it's going?'

'I'm loving it,' I said.

'Is Bruce happy?'

'Very, I'd say.'

'Pace OK?'

'Bowling along.'

'My voice is not what it was. It's breath-y. You'll have noticed?'

'Your voice?'

'I bet you have. Softer.'

'No.'

'I'm fluting a bit. Fading.'

'I didn't notice.'

'Well, I am.'

'You're much the same age as he was. Except he died at 78. So you've outlived him already.'

'Is that meant to be a comfort?'

'A small comfort, and you're coming over perfectly.'

He looked hard at me, trying (I thought) to decide if I was talking guff. As he touched my arm I noticed his right hand was trembling a little, as mine does.

'I'm so glad we're doing this together, Jonathan.'

'Me too.'

'How many of your plays have I been in? Five?'

'Four at the end of this.'

45 | THE SUNDAY SERVICE, 1977

He could feel the tingling in his upper arm, starting just below his right shoulder, a tingling current that ran right down his bicep and forearm to the ends of his fingers, his slowing, recalcitrant, fumbly fingers. In a slight panic he tried to focus on his immediate surroundings. He peered round the nave and the chancel and at the rood screen and up at the roof, trying to find comfort in familiarity, and then back down at the heavily embroidered altar cloth. Or were there two altar cloths?

Because he was also having a bit of eye trouble. He was having some double vision, which had been getting worse for a while. In fact, now he came to think of it, more or less everything on the health front had been getting worse. But he was damned if he was going to start doing jigsaws and crosswords to keep himself alert, or, as the doctors liked to put it, to help keep your brain active, Sir John. He would rather meet His Maker in a blurry state than die clear-headed while doing a fucking jigsaw.

As an optical test, he tried to make out the numbers of the hymns up on the board behind the pulpit. Was that number an 8 or was that number a 3? It was an 8. No, it was a 3. In truth he wasn't sure which, and the more he concentrated on the numbers on the board the less confident he was, but fortunately the moment the congregation stood up to sing a hymn he didn't have to worry because as soon as he heard the first few words of the first line he knew them all by heart. *Hymns Ancient and Modern*, Hymns Happy and Hymns Sad, Addison or Wesley or Watts, whoever wrote it, the whole world of hymnody was in his DNA.

As he looked slowly round he gave himself a Pull-Yourself-Together. He looked at the pews to his front and to his side. He couldn't turn round and check the pew right behind because his creaking neck was far too stiff for that particular manoeuvre. That's why reversing the car in the driveway at home was now completely out of the question; he'd lost count of the shrubs he had flattened and the potted geraniums he had reduced to archaeological rubble. In truth, his whole body was beyond a joke.

Anyway, the most cursory of glances made it clear that there wasn't much of a turn-out in church. Even by modern standards this was a thin Christian witness, with just the usual suspects, the usual quavering voices, the singing a little bit ragged, a congregation of about fifteen Cornish souls in all. One of them, one he'd never spotted before, was blonde and full-bodied and windblown. A bonus. He started to count this happy band of pilgrims.

Fifteen, sixteen of them, if you included the vicar.

Seventeen with the organist.

Plus the verger: hidden away somewhere, as usual.

Each Sunday morning these Trebetherick locals trudged to church, summoned in a slow trickle down Daymer Lane and past the sloping car park and across the edge of the golf course, summoned to St Enodoc by the tinny, tenor bell. And each Sunday, whatever the weather, man and boy, he had done his loyal best to join in the worship.

The dear old Church of England, he had always loved it and he always would, whatever Penelope said or did. But, try as he might, during the sermon these days his mind would switch off and go elsewhere. It especially did so during these middle-stumper sermons, when he found himself wandering willy-nilly the lanes of his past life. His memories were like bicycle bells suddenly ringing behind you in the road and coming up fast and taking you by surprise, bells ringing let-me-pass, remember-the-past, remember your father, Ernest, how can you ever forget him, remember your son, Paul, how can you ever forget him, and then there were the distant church bells coming over the Camel Estuary from Padstow, waves of bells, bell notes rebounding, like sea spray blowing backwards, building a high tide of memories, bells too many and strong.

That particular Sunday he feared he was losing his grip as well as his balance. He feared he was going at the edges. There were – he ought to face it – increasing signs that he was now sitting in the outpatients' department of Purgatory. Tap him too hard and he could well fall apart, like a jigsaw in a box. Not, of course, that he had got any jigsaws.

He slowly turned his neck, his creaking neck, very slightly to the right and as he did so he caught his breath. His chest tightened. There she was, the love of his life. Elizabeth. Feeble. His Elizabeth, or My Feeble as he liked to call her. He could feel her warmth. He could smell the scent on her hair. Her body was there and his body was right there next to her in the pew and so, thank God, were his senses. But his mind was not. And his spirit was not.

However hard he tried to be alive and present in that church on that Sunday morning, he was all over the show: he was everywhere but there. He was back teaching at that prep school in Middlesex or he was back as a new bug with buck teeth at Marlborough, back with a shudder at Marlborough (motto, One kiss and you go!), a basket case, breathing the smell of warm gym shoes and margarine and carbolic soap. Or he was up at Oxford, only to see the unforgiving face of C.S. Lewis, his hard-boiled tutor, Heavy Lewis, glaring across the room at him.

C.S. Lewis.

Your essay, Betjeman? Yet again, Betjeman, I do not appear to have your essay. You cannot just swan into a tutorial, Betjeman, and this late, and with nothing to show for it. Or is it simply that you like to provoke and shock, Betjeman? You have to be different, don't you? You have to be a character. I can't work out whether you're a natural clown, Betjeman, or whether you live purely for effect.

He needed C.S. Lewis psycho-analysed out of him. High time he cleared away all that baggage. It had gone on far too long.

He half closed his eyes.

John dear?

Yes.

If you close your eyes, do make sure your mouth doesn't fall open.

Yes, Feeble. Sorry, my love.

The vicar was still going on, still frowning down at them, sinners all, sinners each and every one. The parson in the pulpit in his horn-rimmed glasses. Such a bore.

Do give him the benefit of the doubt, John.

So he tried again to listen. Dutifully. But he couldn't.

Don't think of death.

You'll have to co-operate with The Inevitable soon enough. Better to think of those days when things were full of promise. So, Sir John, sit quietly in your pew, resting your tired old eyes, until some happy thoughts come back to you. That's better, Happy Families, yes, playing cards together, that's better. Remember that card game we used to play, *Happy Families* it was called, that *was* fun, wasn't it… Playing cards round the dining room table when we *were* a family, The Propellor and The Powlie and Wibbly-Wobbly and I. You had to ask for a card with formulaic politeness, you had to say *Please may I* before each request and you had to say thank you after you had been handed the card. It was very good for your manners, and manners were jolly important, especially if you were middle class. Please may I have Mr Test the Teacher? Thank you. Please may I have Mr Stamp the Postman?

You didn't say thank you!

Yes, I did!

No, you didn't! Give it back!

Children, *chil-dren*!

He was breathing more steadily now, the tingling in his arm was less pronounced and he was settling down to a cosy warm-hearted film: he was watching the two of them, young Paul and young Candida, racing along the wide sands of Daymer Bay, with high-pitched shrieks and cartwheels, with bubbles of fizzy lemonade on their lips, while he sat with a rope around his mackintosh on a sea-weedy rock, on a rock veined green and purple, sitting in his sodden trousers, looking at the surf line, the long tide-mark in the sand.

Sand in the sandwiches, wasps in the tea...

Only he wasn't sitting on a sea-weedy rock on their family hols and there weren't wasps in the tea and the young Paul and the young Candida weren't racing along Daymer Bay because he was at morning service in St Enodoc church and there was a hassocky smell and the vicar was still up there in his pulpit and still going strong while son Paul, The Powlie, had become a Mormon and was playing his saxophone and as for his wife, Penelope...

Oh God.

He closed his eyes, as if *that* was going to help.

He could see his wife, closed eyes or no closed eyes.

Penelope.

Or Lady Penelope, as she now was. Where on earth was she?

The last he heard from her she was in India. She had written him one of her long, newsy letters. Penelope was good like that. She wrote such gossipy, long, newsy, personal letters, because she was happier when she was off with her horses and sitting on her shiny saddle. Was it from Jaipur, her last letter, wherever Jaipur was? No, it was from much further north, from somewhere up in the Himalayas. Anyway, she was somewhere in India, on horseback, her skin leathery from the sun, happily many thousands of miles away from her husband who was in a bit of a state, filling up with guilt in his Cornish pew, rather like the Camel estuary filling up with the sea.

Dear God.

He lowered his head, as he so often did, chin on his chest, and screwed his eyes tight and pulled the plug on the sermon, putting his hands together in silent prayer.

Dear Lord, I acknowledge my transgressions and my sins are ever before me. On my knees I pray. Not that I can now get down on my knees. In fact I can't bend down at all. In truth, I am a faintly-ticking clock. All I can do is lower my head and close my eyes and thank you for the lives of my children, *our* children rather, Paul and Candida, and for our grandchildren.

And above all I thank you for Elizabeth, who is beside me now, Elizabeth, who lives with me, who lives with me in sin, Elizabeth otherwise known as Feeble though she is anything but feeble, because like all the very best people in life she has a soft front but a strong back, Elizabeth who has so loyally loved me and given up her life for me since 1951. Dear Lord, I am very sorry for all my transgressions. I am not a good man. I may even be a bad man.

He peeped to his right. Yes, Elizabeth was still there.

He felt safe with her. Occasionally she would squeeze his trembly hand or lock her fingers in his. She had the most lovely hands. Hands were very important. Touch was very important, and even more so when one became older: when you were old you couldn't put a price on kind hands and kind arms. Feeble nudged him if he nodded off in his pew or anywhere in public or if he made his little tell-tale-snort-and-jolt as his head jerked down on to his chest. If he slumped heavily sideways she gently but firmly eased him back to an upright position.

He loved to lean on her as he could then feel her warmth coming back into him through his jacket. Oh, how he loved her. Where on earth would he be without her? He even loved the way she pointed out that there were some white bristles on his chin, the little bits he had missed while shaving.

After the service, all being well, he would, once again – while Feeble went off to cook the lunch – sit for a while on the bench, alone, on the bench at the top of the churchyard, his bench, if you would excuse him being proprietorial. And once he was up there, he would have a quiet think about his latest idea, *Spots of Time*, an idea which had been swirling around in his mind and which was even beginning to take some sort of shape in his pocket notebook. Not that he was at all keen to be seen Wordsworthying around the place. Despite repeated pressure from his publishers, he did not want to write an autobiography and (whatever the money) he was not going to write one, thank you very much. There was too much to hide. Let others rip themselves open like a pig. But *Spots of Time* had some appeal, if he could find the energy, if only there were enough petrol left in the writing tank.

Spots of time. Snapshots. Memories. That's what things had come to.

It was a risky business, though, lifting up the stones of your past life to see what had been lying hidden underneath, thinking back to being a son and being a father, to all that went wrong, never knowing what would come crawling out or where it all might lead. Why lift up the stones of your past life for millions to see, why risk it, why let them delve into your soul, which is always dangerous if your soul is troubled and your conscience troublesome?

It wasn't as if the past could be put right. It wasn't like fixing the radiators.

Being filmed on the telly, he often felt, was a bit like undressing in public and showing your parts. On the other hand, he had to admit, it was thanks to the telly that he was rich. That he could run a house in Chelsea and this house in Daymer Lane. That his books sold. That he could drink champagne from a pewter mug at lunchtime. Ay, there's the rub. Instead of scraping up a press-ganged audience in a village hall all he had to do now was plonk himself in front of a camera and have a chinwag. It was money for jam, money for old rope. Sometimes one has to do second-rate things one doesn't want to do so that one can do the things one wants to.

And if he ever did decide to let it all come out he certainly wouldn't be telling anyone what he was up to. Not even Elizabeth. And he rather liked that too, because being a bit subversive came naturally to him, being (as he was) a bit of a spy.

Whether it led anywhere or not, whether anything came of it, when the service was over he would look out to Stepper Point and Doom Bar and The Atlantic. A flat sea, a consoling sea, a ruffled sea, a tossed sea, a foaming sea, he knew all the ocean's moods. And there hadn't been a year of his life, flat or ruffled or foaming, when he hadn't been there, when he hadn't sat there, an emotional wreck, washed up on that very spot.

D addy, come and watch me!'
    'In a minute.'
  'Watch me do somersaults.'
  'I'm busy.'
  'I can do three in a row.'
  'Gosh, can you? Some-*er*-saults?'
  'And I can do a handstand. Daddy, watch me! And I can hold it. Like this.'
  'Is that a hand-stand?'
  'Candida can't do a handstand. You do one with me. Please.'

★

However hard he had tried, and in his long life he had tried many times, he had never been able to work it out. Why it was that some moments stuck firmly in the mind, that some days in the distant past were always so clear and so sharp in the memory – re-visited as if they were yesterday – while whole decades, whole swathes of time, had become nothing more than a foggy haze. Why, for example, did some schoolday scenes or some old tunes or the work of some minor writers, read at a certain age or devoured at a certain stage of development, always retain their power?

What was it like being me at those precise moments, what kind of person was I during those spots of time? That's what he was trying to rediscover, that's what he was trying to understand. True, as one gets older, one day is much like the next. Things merge or fold into each other, or seem to. So, was one more alive, more tender, more passionate, more open to suggestion, on some mornings than on others? Worse, much worse, had one already experienced the most exciting parts of one's life by the time one had reached, say, twenty-eight?

That, at least, was what he seemed to believe when he wrote *Summoned By Bells*, which was the closest he'd got – or was ever likely to get – to writing an autobiography.

Take, for instance, that spell of prep school teaching. That was now nearly fifty years ago. And it wasn't as if it was an important post or a significant job. How could it have been when it was a humiliating aberration that added up to just four chequered terms in an antiquated classroom? In 1929 he was only twenty-three, and on the career front things could hardly have been less promising: he was reeling and rudderless from academic failure and from social failure. At twenty-three he was always tying up his boat, weighing things up, and then suddenly deciding to depart, weighing anchor, always setting off from shore but with no clear idea at all where he was going.

It was odd, though, what stuck in the memory and what did not. By rights that whole teaching stint should have been a forgettable farce, one of those embarrassing hiatuses to be silently excised later from one's *curriculum vitae*. Yet he had replayed it endlessly in his mind, and why he wasn't sure, he just couldn't throw it off, round and round it went like a scratchy old record on a wind-up gramophone.

Anyway, for whatever reason, he had accepted it. Some random events did retain a disproportionate intensity, as if the trivial was profound – no, not trivial, never trivial – as if in some unfathomable moments you suddenly held your heart in your hands, like a girl waving to you as she cycles past you on a rutted track or a dragonfly darting by on transparent wings. They sparkled like nuggets, these inexplicable memories. It made no sense, no sense at all.

The latest replaying of the scratched old gramophone record had been triggered when he saw that young boy in his grey flannel suit and his school tie in the front pew. The Poet Laureate liked to sit in the second row, if possible always the second row, he could hear better near the front, and preferably right next to the aisle. Sitting next to the aisle also made it much easier when it came to manoeuvring his legs, quite apart for his paunch, making it less trouble than squeezing in or clambering past someone and knocking over *Hymns Ancient and Modern* or *The Book of Common Prayer.*

Anyway, this particular boy in the grey flannel suit had reminded him a bit of Paul, son Paul. Just a bit. No, more than a bit. Perhaps it was his thin neck? More likely it was his haircut and his eyelashes which were noticeable when the boy (perhaps as bored by the sermon as the bald old buffer behind him) turned to look at the commemorative plaque on the south wall of the nave. Did his schoolboy's eyes catch the wording of the dedication? *Sacred to the memory of Ernest Edward Betjemann of Undertown in this parish, born 22 October 1872, died 22 June 1934.*

There was a distinct resemblance in his profile, no doubt about that, and then it all came flooding back, uncontrollably, the hopes he had felt for Paul when he was a chatterbox of a boy with his oval-shaped head and his fair, tousled hair. Nut-shaped, oval-shaped, fair hair, long eyelashes. The similarity was uncanny. Memory hurts if you touch it in certain places. If only he could stand up on the kitchen chair and prise the clock off the wall, the clock sticky with cooking fat, and turn back the years and do things better. Oh, if only he could put things right. How could anyone who has lived any kind of life at all honestly say he has no regrets? You have *no* regrets? Honestly?

And talking of which, in his worst dreams his son was one of the boys in that prep school classroom. The pupils were all looking up and laughing (with mouths wide open) at his music hall jokes and *double entendres* as he performed and promenaded and swirled and strutted back and forth on the dais. All except Paul. In his worst dreams Paul was always staring down at his desk, carving his name deeply on it with a sharp penknife. There was animus in his isolation and hatred in his hunched shoulders and violence in the way he dug his penknife into the wood.

I can never forget that sentence in Arnold Bennett, forgotten which novel, about Cyril, the son. *He had settled down into a dilettante, having learnt gently to scorn the triumphs which he lacked the force to win.*

As for calling you silly names, the teasing and the taunting, Egghead and so forth – which worries me to this day – that was a private game between your mother and me. It was our *faux bonhomie*, our kind of togetherness, the only kind we had left when everything else had gone. With us there was only going to church and mockery. Then when your mother crossed over to Rome there was just mockery, nothing left but swift sallies of wit.

Anyway, you got a 4th in Geography at Oxford and I got sent down. I'm not sure which is worse.

47 | WOMAN IN THE CHURCHYARD

I'm sorry to bother you, but are you Sir John Betjeman?'
The outline of a woman was there, only a few yards from his seat.

'I am, yes. Sorry, I was miles away.'

'No, I stole up on you, but I said to myself that's Sir John Betjeman, that is, I've seen him on the television, but I didn't like to ask.'

'That's quite all right.'

'I hope I'm not being rude, but it's just that I really like your poems. And I always have. And I wanted to say that.'

His eyes had cleared a bit. He could now see her.

'Thank you.'

'They make me feel proud.'

He sat up a bit, not sure he had heard her correctly.

'Do they? In what way?'

'Proud to be Cornish. And I just wanted to tell you.'

'Oh, how wonderful, I couldn't ask for anything better. No one's ever said that to me before.'

'I read them to myself at night, not every night, mind, but most nights. Our headmaster back at primary school made us learn poems by heart. *The Donkey* by G.K. Chesterton, that was one. And I tried to learn one of yours, but it wouldn't stick. Sorry, that sounds a bit rude.'

'Not a bit. Do sit down.'

'No, I'd better not, thank you, I've got the church to do now everyone has gone.'

'Are you from around here?'

'Yes. St Minver.'

'Oh, not far.'

'Every Tuesday I come on the bus, to give the church a good clean. And some Sundays.'

'Do you?'

'And I always notice your mother's grave by the wall.'

'Yes, that's the one. If you stand next to it you can hear the golfers teeing off.'

'It's very close to my daughter's. Three along.'

'Your daughter's?'

'Sometimes I miss a week, which I shouldn't, I mean it's not asking a lot, is it, a few flowers to say she's not forgotten.'

'No, no, it's not.'

'And I like to come and sit here. To be with her. She loved running along the beach in her bare feet, right the way from the car park to the end of Daymer Bay, and then back.'

'Did she? So did my two.'

'I can see her now, clear as day. Still, can't be helped. Can I just ask you something?'

'Please.'

'Is it right that you came here to church with your parents? Because that's what people say.'

'Yes, every Sunday, the three of us. Never missed, come rain or shine.'

'And then you came with your children?'

'That's right, we did. Every week. Whoever the vicar was!'

'Oh, I know, we've had all sorts of vicars here. Some of them try to change everything, and only make it worse. I like things the way they were, but they just can't leave it alone, can they?'

'But what matters, at the end of the day, is that it's our church, isn't it?'

'Yes, it's our church, that's right. Ours.'

'And always will be.'

'Is your father buried here too? Because I polish his brass plate in the church.'

'That's kind of you. No, he's buried in Highgate cemetery. In North London.'

'Oh. Oh. Well, never mind.'

'But I hope to be buried here myself.'

'Do you!'

'Just down there, there's a nice spot. By the lych gate.'

'There is. That is a nice spot.'

'And, like you, I always come and sit here... when things are a bit too much.'

'I know what you mean. Anyway, I'd better be off.'

'You've given me a lot to think about. Hope to meet you again.'

'Goodbye.'

'And thank you.'

John? John!'

He can hear that long-loved voice, her voice, the voice he lives with, but he can't yet see her. It's Feeble coming up, it's Elizabeth Cavendish, an elegant woman, a cut above.

'John? John!'

She's down there, by the church porch.

'Yes, up here, Elizabeth. On the bench.'

'*Com*-ing. I went to get your hat.'

She waved, a cheerily open wave, the wave of an innocent girl. It stabbed him to the heart, her wave, it always did, and he always said it's the heart that matters. It left him winded, wilting, weak. He waved back. They had these little rituals, these little courtesies, as if they were still young lovers.

I'm her slave, all right, he mumbled, I'm drunk with her, and he had been since the night they first met at that dinner party in Lord North Street. 1951. It was a night he would never forget, the night Guy Burgess did not turn up for the simple reason that he had defected to Russia. The traitor. You never would have guessed that Guy Burgess would betray his country, though you could argue that being at Eton and Trinity, Cambridge was a bit of a give-away, but then that presumably was the whole point with spies, they were the last people you would think were spies. Any spy worthy of the name would, he imagined, aim to be unreadable.

Anyway, there at the table Elizabeth was, and there was the traitor's place left empty beside her. He did not know she was Lady Elizabeth Cavendish, the daughter of the Duke of Devonshire, let alone Princess Margaret's Lady-in-Waiting, but he could not stop looking at her. They did not speak to each other at any stage that evening, and they did not need to.

If ever two were one, then surely we. For both of them that simple line was a simple truth. Everything was perfect from the moment they set eyes on each other, except for the guilt, and except that he was married and twenty years older and there was no question of him ever getting a divorce from Penelope.

49 | PERSHORE STATION

The train at Pershore station was waiting that Sunday night,
Gas light on the platform, in my carriage electric light,
Gas light on frosty evergreens, electric on Empire wood,
The Victorian world and the present in a moment's neighbourhood.
There was no one about but a conscript who was saying good-bye
   to his love
On the windy weedy platform with the sprinkled stars above
When sudden the waiting stillness shook with the ancient spells
Of an older world than all our worlds in the sound of the Pershore
   bells.
They were ringing them down for Evensong in the lighted abbey
   near,
Sounds which had poured through apple boughs for seven centuries
   here.
With Guilt, Remorse, Eternity the void within me fills
And I thought of her left behind me in the Herefordshire hills.
I remembered her defencelessness as I made my heart a stone
Till she wove her self-protection round and left me on my own.
And plunged in a deep self pity I dreamed of another wife
And lusted for freckled faces and lived a separate life.
One word would have made her love me, one word would have
   made her turn
But the word I never murmured and now I am left to burn.
Evesham, Oxford and London. The carriage is new and smart.
I am cushioned and soft and heated with a deadweight in my heart.

Now he sees what Feeble is carrying.

'Ah, how kind.'

'What a scorcher!'

'Isn't it? Oh, you found that old one. My Harrow boater.'

'Harrow?'

'Yes.'

'I didn't know it was Harrow.'

'Oh yes.'

'But you weren't at Harrow.'

'No, I wasn't. I pinched it. Well, I borrowed it.' He did his naughty boy mock-whisper, 'And I've got a Harrow first eleven sweater somewhere as well.'

'I left the hat for you by the front door, dear.'

'Did you?'

'Didn't you see it?'

''Fraid I didn't.'

She was sitting next to him, on his left, looking at the ocean.

'Two calls on the blower for you.'

'Only two?'

'Some girl, to remind you of your interview tomorrow. That's at three.'

'*The Sunday Magazine*, yes, yes, why do they keep on reminding me?'

'Perhaps it's because you keep on forgetting.'

Ah, that most remote of times, the recent past.

'And I don't give a damn what they write about me as long as it isn't true. Tell you what, I'll read them some Kipling. That'll annoy them.'

'And you'll never guess who else rang.'

'Who?'

'All the way from America.'

His mouth opened a little and stayed open. Old habits die

hard, particularly with Parkinson's.

'Not Paul?'

'Yes, from New York.'

'Why? What for?'

'Wanted a word with you.'

'Did he?'

'Hence the telephone. And he's ringing again later.'

She took his hand.

'Paul,' he mumbled.

'Paul.'

He swallowed. She went on,

'He's flying over this week and wants to see you.'

'From New York?'

'I assume so, but he didn't mention that.'

'To see me? He said that?'

'Yes, isn't it lovely?'

'When exactly this week?

'On Wednesday. He'd like to come down here.'

'That's... Did he really?'

'Yes.'

'Down *here*? To Trebetherick? Not Chelsea?'

'That's what he said. Don't put Dad out, he said.'

'Well, there's a thing.'

He took out his spotted handkerchief and wiped the sweat off his forehead and his scalp and stared at his dusty toe caps. He then tried to rub his right toe cap on the back of his trousers. And failed. He was sticky with sweat. Again, he wiped his head with his handkerchief. The sky was now milkier, the light less sharp. Or was that his failing eyes?

'So... another unannounced arrival... before... another unannounced departure.'

'John –'

'That's Paul.'

'John.'

'That is The Egg for you.'

'But he's just announced it. He's telephoned us, or you rather, to ask.'

'Leaving us no time to say no.'

'But you don't want to say no, do you?'

'No. But it's unsettling, coming out of the blue. Surely you can see that! Or is it all too difficult for you to grasp?'

Feeble looked straight ahead, already counting to ten.

'Oh, and he's bringing a friend. Not to worry about beds, he said, they'll be staying in a hotel. In Wadebridge.'

'A friend?'

'Yes.'

'They don't have to stay in a hotel. We've got enough room.'

'I told him that. But he – and his friend – have obviously decided.'

'Did he say who it was, this friend?'

'No.'

He tried to moisten his dry lips. His eyes began to panic. She said,

'I thought you'd be pleased.'

'Oh, I am, I am.'

'Because you've been mentioning him a lot lately.'

'Sounding more American by the minute, was he?'

'Not that I noticed. Mind you, I wouldn't know, we've never met and hardly ever spoken. He's your son, not mine.'

'Yes yes, no need to make a meal of it, I'm quite well aware of –'

'Well, you haven't been in touch with him yourself for five years.'

'Five years!'

'At least.'

'It's never five years!'

'It's time you put all that behind you, long past time. You

don't want to take it with you –'

'To my grave, you mean?'

'You've said it yourself. And Penelope has said it. You must get together, you and Paul, and the sooner the better. Are you all right?'

'Yes. Yes.'

'You're looking a little bit flustered, that's all.'

'Because I'm hot,' he snapped.

She turned to look at him.

'So, put your hat on then. You haven't had one of your funny turns, have you?'

'No.'

'Because I'm not sure I'm convinced by those new pills.'

'The doctor said they take a week or so to kick in.'

'And he also said to cut down on the drink, cut down on the interviews, cut down on –'

'Did he say cut down on interviews?'

'He said cut down full stop. Mind you, I have to say you were jolly good with Michael Parkinson.'

'Was I?'

'Very funny. And it went down awfully well.'

'Not with the critics, I bet. For them I'm just a donkey ride, a comma in the wrong place.'

'Who cares about them? They're simply jealous of your recognition. I'm talking about the general public, your readers, and they absolutely loved it.'

'Did they? Oh, you are sweet. Snuggle up.'

'No, I meant it. I don't say things I don't mean.'

'Oh I do all the time. Otherwise life is quite impossible.'

She laughed.

'Yes, John dear, I know all that. Just don't let your guard down too much.'

'You mean, don't let them give the sauce bottle another shake? Don't you worry, I won't.'

'You may be an old hand at it, but you are prone to show off a bit, and then things slip out.'

'Which might be the pills.'

'Or the drink.'

'Do you always have to mention that!'

Elizabeth stood up.

'Instead of sitting here letting yourself get low why don't you think of all the things you've achieved?'

'But I've always been afraid of being found out.'

'Found out as the poet who sells like hot cakes, who sells more than any other poet? Found out as the Poet Laureate, a household name? Everyone wants to hear you talk, because you inspire people and make them feel loved and touch their hearts and give them courage in their campaigns, and you save churches and railway stations. You make everyone feel they're your chief *confidant*. Which comes all too easily to you, you clever old thing.'

'Gosh, not sure I like the sound of that.'

'And you make people's day better, and because you make them feel special, that makes the world a better place, and, on top of all that, you're greatly loved.'

'You're my fireside fan club. Come here.'

'No, it annoys me.'

51 | THE GREEN ROOM, 2017

Around tea time, with four more scenes safely in the can, I went up into the Green Room, where I found Sarah Crowden (Penelope), Joanna David (Elizabeth) and Ben sitting together. They seemed to be deep in a private chat on the long sofa so I hovered at the door. Joanna David stood up.

'Jonathan, a cup of tea?'

'Is that OK?'

'I'd avoid the coffee.'

'I'm not barging in?'

'Not a bit,' Sarah said. 'Join us. We're talking about our first kiss.'

'OK.'

'When was yours?' Ben asked me.

'Mine?'

'At least let him sit down first,' Sarah said.

'Sit down, and then tell us,' Joanna said.

'No,' I said, 'not in front of you lot. You're the actors.'

'We're not acting.'

'We want to know.'

'Jonathan, spill the beans.'

They all nodded in gang-up unison and raised their eyebrows and applied pressure. Joanna handed me a carton cup of BBC tea and sat back, body language expectant. So, I gave them an edited version. My first kiss? It took place in the Tivoli Cinema, Mumbles, Swansea, or 'In the Tiv' as we called it. Back row. This was in 1956 or '57. I was staying in West Cross, in a *cul-de-sac* on the bay.

I remember I looked at the clock on the cinema wall and to steel my resolve I said to myself, as a challenge, right, I'm going to make my move at five o'clock, the moment the clock hits five. I would have been fifteen, fourteen, anyway a late starter. She was lovely and eager. She was called Sally. Or was it Sarah?

In truth I was a bit put off my stride by the question because the first girl I had ever kissed happened a few months earlier, and it was in the back of a coach on a church outing to the seaside, to Weston-super-Mare, one of Betjeman's places as luck would have it, indeed the whole thing was Betjeman, but I didn't want to go into any of this, not so much because the kiss had been (for her) a one-sided unwelcome affair but because at school a few months later she was hit on the head by a hockey ball and died. She was good at hockey. I went to visit her in hospital and I sat on the end of her bed and we had a nice chat and she seemed fine. Next thing I heard, that was it. She was called Penny and I used to stand in front of her grave in the churchyard, on your right as you walk down the path towards the west door at Almondsbury, and I would stop, confused, in a blur of unfocused questions, not knowing what to make of it, and last year I stood there again, sixty years on but no further forward.

'Have you ever seen her since?'

'Who?'

'The girl in the cinema. Sally Whatshername.'

'Only the next day. At the bus stop. I felt so proud of myself.'

'Was it just the one kiss?' Ben asked.

'No, God no.'

Having lied, I sipped my tea.

I run my fingers down your dress
With brandy-certain aim,
And you respond to my caress
And maybe feel the same.

'I'm still taken aback in films, usually American films,' I said, 'when girls take their clothes off in a very matter of fact let's get on with it way. Probably my problem. Sorry, it's not a very exciting story. What about you, Ben? What about your first kiss?'

'I can't remember,' he said. 'I can remember my first fuck.'

★

Safely back in the control cubicle, Bruce turned to ask me about the music we were going to use. We'd emailed each other about it in earlier weeks and I had put a few markers down, a few feelers, Handel's *Ombra Mai Fu*, Kathleen Ferrier kind of thing, no, no, too obvious, it makes me cry, what's wrong with that, but you want to keep an open mind because during the recording you often have new thoughts or your feelings about the overall tone of the drama may change.

It was appropriate to be thinking about music in Maida Vale studios because just off the ill-lit corridors the BBC Symphony orchestra were at full throttle rehearsing Mahler (I think) as I walked past. In earlier days the music for radio drama was often put on tape during the studio recording with the actors but now it is usually done during the editing.

When you think of Betjeman and music two main worlds of sound come to mind. Hymns and Music Hall. Hymns, any number of hymns, the Anglican faith, Anglican choirs, Anglican church music, communal and solo, *Dear Lord and Father of Mankind*, *The Church's One Foundation*, *Fight the Good Fight* and *Now the Day is over*, or you can hear, if you really try, on a cold winter's night on the Berkshire Downs, the treble voice of Paul Betjeman singing the solo in *Once in Royal David's City*.

Ninety-seven of Betjeman's published poems, one third of his output, are concerned with church or religion. Even if Christians in this country are an endangered species, indeed especially if they are, I have (in the plays) to honour his religious sensibility, his commitment and his example.

Then there's his Music Hall side. Although Music Hall (or Variety) was on its last legs well before Betjeman was, he adored Vesta Tilley, the male impersonator, the female drag king, jolly good luck to the girl who loves a soldier, and you can't really watch any of the old timers on stage singing *Boiled Beef and Carrots* without seeing an image of Betjeman roaring with laughter.

On Desert Island Discs he chose, of course, Harrow schoolboys singing *Ducker*, or, jumping sideways, Ella Fitzgerald's *Let's Do It*, which brings us, more or less, to jazz. Like Larkin, though less seriously, he loved jazz. It might be tea room jazz, or quirky jazz, or working with Jim Parker on the *Banana Blush* LP, Parker's musical settings of thirteen poems on the Charisma label, and Betjeman's taste on the sax might have run to the lugubrious Ben Webster but it would never have stretched to John Coltrane's bebop and hard bop.

Paul Betjeman played the saxophone, played it well, and Paul loved John Coltrane. Even when it came to jazz father and son were on different wavelengths.

52 | THE PHONE CALL

My phone went that night at 11.15. It was a voice I knew well, the Scottish sound of Carrie Gibbons, Bruce Young's PA. I was sitting on the end of my bed, reading.

'Jonathan?'

'Yes, Carrie.'

'I didn't wake you up?'

'No, it's fine.'

In fact I was ploughing my way through the Yorks and Lancasters in *Henry VI Part 3*, another hurdle in my determination to read, for the first time, the collected works of Shakespeare.

'I'm afraid I have some bad news.'

'Yes?'

'Ben Whitrow has had a fall at home. He's in hospital.'

'God. Really?'

'I'm sorry, Jonathan, but it's very serious. And I know you're friends.'

'But we had lunch together. A fall? Where is he? Where have they taken him?'

'St George's, Tooting. In intensive care.'

'My God.'

'I hear it's a great hospital. That's about all I know.'

'Please ring when you hear any more. Any time, Carrie. If you hear any more. Any time.'

I could feel Ben's hand in mine, light, surprisingly light, and warm, as we shook hands after the last session of the third day.

'Of course I will,' Carrie said.

'I'll see you in the morning, Carrie.'

'I'll be there.'

'And thank you for telling me.'

★

I must have dozed a bit but mainly I lay in the dark, apart from a spell with the bedside light on, taking what little comfort that light can bring. I tried to read but couldn't. Around four I went down to make a cup of tea. I sat in the kitchen, stirring the tea, and ate a banana. Later, much later, back in bed, I saw hints of dawn outline the curtains. Could Ben see it in Tooting?

There was, I had noticed but not fully admitted to myself, something wrong with him yesterday in the studio. I knew there was but I didn't want to face it. I saw the panic in his eyes, that vulnerability, that fear of collapsing just before he crossed the finishing line, the sense that he was clinging on, just about there but only just, only just in control of whatever was left, and what was left of him was his talent.

And I lay there, propped on my pillows, clinging on to myself, frightened too, frightened that this would tip me back, back to the place that I had taken so long to haul myself out from.

I'm not going back there. Not if I can help it. No good comes from being there. Whatever else, don't go back there. No spiralling down, no bad buses. This is not a bus you are getting on. Ben and I know about bad buses and about wreckage. I am not being swept away by a river, like driftwood, like flotsam. I kept closing my eyes, trying to close it all out, but the jabbering grew, the mad monkeys.

Enough.

I got up and had a shower. As I stood in the bathroom I knew Ben was going to die, may even have died. I knew it in my bones. I sat on the laundry box by the sink and spoke to him. I said I was with him. I told him he was lovely to be with, because you are, Ben, you are. You were. You are.

★

The control room in the studio was empty when I got into Maida Vale. The Tonbridge to Charing Cross train was on time and the Bakerloo line was normal. In fact, after the ten minute walk from Warwick Road tube, I was more than a bit early.

I tried the Green Room, the canteen, all the places someone might be. All empty. My left arm started to tick. My feet were heavy. Had the day been cancelled when I was on the train? No, they wouldn't do that. Carrie or Bruce would have rung me.

I sat in the reception area and checked the script of the second play. I calculated – I didn't like myself for doing so but I couldn't help it – I calculated there was about a half of it left to do; some big scenes for Betjeman not to mention the whole sense of an ending. In the read-through, though frail, Ben had done all that so well, so naturally. You have to get the ending right. Perhaps, though, there was to be no right ending here.

I stood up. I could not settle. But I decided against ringing

Bruce. He had enough on his plate. Instead I spent another fifteen minutes going up and down the narrow corridors from one place to another, until, at my third visit, I found Bruce and Joanna David and Sarah Crowden and Carrie together in the Green Room. We all hugged. Carrie told me that Ben was on life support.

'Those bloody stairs of his,' Sarah said. 'I told him. I've forgotten how many times I've told him.'

I remembered the stairs, how steep they were in his book-lined house in Wimbledon. I remembered his small kitchen and how much he liked his roasted potatoes. And smoked salmon, of course. And a hard-boiled egg.

'Terrible coffee,' Joanna said, putting down her plastic cup.

After a while Bruce got to his feet and looked round at us, 'Let's do whatever bits we can, shall we?' Carrie and I followed him down through the studio to the control room.

★

At lunchtime Bruce and I wandered off to find a café, any café. Although nearly October it was fine enough to sit at a table on the pavement, though we were the only ones to do so. Bruce, staring ahead, smoked a cigarette. He did not eat at all and I did not want to eat but for some flustered reason, for something to do, I ordered a club sandwich. After a few attempts I gave up. The chicken might as well have been cardboard.

Ben was gone. He wasn't here.

Bruce was lost in thought, his eyes either on his mobile or on the middle distance, and there was nothing more we could do back in the studio. But, wordless though I may have been, I did not want to walk along to the tube and go home. I wanted to be there, with company, in the intensifying silence.

I could hear Ben's light voice. I could feel his light hand.

'Give me a while to have a talk,' Bruce said, lighting

another cigarette. 'A few weeks. See what they say, see what the options are.'

'Right.'

'There's a lot to consider.'

I didn't need to ask what the options were as I was, despite myself, now going over them. Play one was complete. Did we settle for that, be grateful for what we'd got, cut our losses and write off play two, bad luck, everyone, nothing we could do, just one of those things. That seemed the likeliest move. Or did we, if new money were to be available, cast a new actor and start again with play two, do the whole second play from scratch?

But having listened to what Ben had already done with the first half of the second play, did we really want to ditch that wonderful final performance? Or – the most risky and least likely option – we could re-group, re-order the scenes, and cast a new actor to take up the reins halfway through the second play? Could anyone do that? Should anyone do that?

53 | PAUL

The Poet Laureate's eyes were closed but his nose twitched. Is he in his pew or is he on his bench? When he is on his bench he feels he is in his pew. When he is in church his mind wanders off among the tombstones and he smells things that aren't there. Turkish cigarettes (Balkan Sobranies). Irish stew. The sooty remains in an unlit summer's fireplace. A rubbery over-hot hot-water bottle. Cheroots. A slice of lemon in the gin. A soapy bath. A dank, airless cave.

Oh, his eyesight might be going and his legs might be gone, but his sense of smell was still the keenest, even when it came to imagined ones. For instance, if he wrote down the word 'plasticine' he could immediately smell the sticky putty stuff. And just thinking about the phrase 'buttered toast' could make him start to drool and leak a little at the corners of his mouth.

He half-opened one eye in the sun's stare and looked past the crooked spire (so like a witch's hat) and out to sea, the same old sea which was different every minute of every day. You can't beat the Cornwall coastline. Some days it made him dotty with happiness: to be in a Cornish church he loved with the woman he loved in a part of Cornwall he loved, what more could he want? On these rare occasions of contentment even complicated things seem clear.

★

'John. You've nodded off again.'

He tried to open his eyes, but they only flickered and stayed shut. His eyelids now had a mind of their own.

'Yes, Feeble.'

His mouth was dry. He forced his eyelids partly open, then more open to the colour-shafted air.

'You say you love being with me but you keep falling asleep. Are we ready to go?'

'Go where?'

'Home for lunch. Time to take you. Everyone's gone. And the vicar's just left.'

'Gosh, sorry.'

'He knew you were up here but didn't want to disturb you. He asked me to say goodbye and to say he would see you next week.'

Coming fully to his senses, he looked round and lowered his voice to what he wrongly thought a whisper,

'Terrible sermon, wasn't it?'

'Wasn't it!'

'So dull. Terrible! So worthy.'

'Shhh. Too loud. The verger's still about.'

'Ooops.'

'Shall we be off then?'

She turned to face him. His left hand drummed the side of the bench. One corner of his mouth was turned up. He had his guilty grin on.

'You're up to something, John. I know you. You are, aren't you? You can't fool me.'

'Nothing much, guv, honest. I'm a pretty empty-headed old buffer.'

'Don't play games. I can read you like a book. What are you thinking about?'

'Oh, funny things from the past, that kind of thing, how I got things so wrong.'

'Ah.'

'Random stuff, random things off the top of my head.'

'If they're always coming back they're not random. And they may lead you on to something.'

'You think I should write something new?'

'You don't have to. But it would please an awful lot of readers if you did, and you do like pleasing people.'

'I know, I know, I've always been desperate to please.'

'I didn't say that.'

'No, you just thought it.'

He put his shakily apologetic hand on her arm, saying 'I need a drink.'

'And there's that telephone call, remember. To Paul.'

'So there is. And I'm going to, Feeble, believe me, I'm going to.'

'Just make sure you do.'

Telephones crouch, getting ready to ring. Yes, all right, Larkers, all right.

'I've been talking to him. We've had a chat already.'

213

'Who?'

'Paul.'

'You really have been asleep. Up we get. That's it. Get your bearings.'

'Give me a moment, I'll be fine once I'm moving.'

'Do be careful, won't you, on this next bit.'

'It's all right, my dear. I've done it thousands of times.'

'I'm sure you have, but the grass is very slippy.'

'Better give me your arm, then.'

He set off down the slope, down the trampled grass, down the beaten trail, gingerly, the smallest of steps, one at a time.

'How's that?'

'Much better. So cosy. I do like a gel who makes me feel safe.'

'Any gel?'

'My gel, I meant.'

'Mmm.'

'Ooops.'

'*Care*-ful.'

'I'm fine. Fine.'

He isn't.

'Let's go across the fairway. Dodge a few golf balls.'

'If you're up to it.'

They made their way towards the lych gate.

'Did I ever tell you that one about our German *au pair*?'

'I expect so.'

'It's rather… rude.'

'Oh good.'

'Better wait till we're out of sacred ground. Right. Well, once upon a time, many years ago, when The Powlie and Wibz were… no, dammit, when *Paul* and *Candida* were little, and by the way, in case you're in any doubt, Candida and I have always got on –'

'I know that, and it's lovely.'

'Got on famously.'

'So you're not all bad.'

'Anyway we had an *au pair*, a German *au pair*. And she spoke jolly good English, as Germans orfen do, but she was keen to speak more idiomatically, so she kept asking The Propellor and me for colloquial phrases. And one afternoon she came downstairs… No, no, I really shouldn't.'

'You can't stop, not now!'

'Well, she came downstairs and she said she was feeling much better because she'd just had forty wanks.'

'John!'

'True as I'm standing here. Oops, better wait for a sec. That chap's about to play a shot.'

'Which chap? The one in the loud jumper?'

'That's the one. They do like their etiquette, golfers. And their rules. Get on with it! Oh, bad luck, chum. Not your day. Can I confess something?'

'You haven't done enough confessing for one day?'

'The shameful thing is, I've been wondering if there isn't a poem in all this, in all this remorse. Terrible business, being a writer, we're a shocking lot, whatever else is going wrong, you're always writing inside your head. Or I am.'

'Even now?'

'Oh, yes, that loud jumper's in. With no acknowledgement to you of course.'

'Have you been writing all the while, all the while we've been talking?'

'I've got the first verse, more or less. It's corkingly good, even if I say so myself.'

'What's it about?'

'You.'

'It better not be.'

'Yes, you'll be captured for all time. Long after I've gone.'

'Can I hear it?'

'Certainly not. Better move. Look, they're waving us on. We're holding up play again. One more thing.'

'Yes?'

'Might amuse you. When Paul first went to America what did he go and do?'

'Go on.'

'He joined the Church of Jesus Christ of Latter-Day Saints.'

'He became a Mormon?'

'He did. He did indeed. So, Penelope went to Rome, Paul went to Utah, and I stayed in Cornwall.'

54 | THE TRANSATLANTIC PHONE CALL

His right hand was shaking, almost out of control, so he held the receiver as firmly as he could in both hands, while allowing the American ringing tone to continue. He wasn't going to bail out, he wasn't going to cut this one off, not this one, not this time.

–Is that Paul? Hullo, is that Paul?

–Yes?

–Paul?

–Is that Daddy?

–Yes, yes it is. How are you, my boy? Can you hear me?

–Yes, I can hear you.

–The line's bad, very bad.

–Not this end. I can hear you fine. It's a good connection.

–My hearing is not what it was, my boy, in fact I sometimes think I'm nearly as deaf as my poor old dad, well, not –

–Never mind. It's good to hear you. In fact I was about to call you with some news.

–But I got in first.

–Well, you always did.

-Did I?

-Yes. Where are you now? Are you down in Cornwall?

-I am. We are. Been here a fortnight.

-Sounds great.

-We were walking on Daymer Bay this morning. Some big seas. Well, you'd know about all that. I say, I haven't woken you up, have I?

-Not a bit. We're five hours behind you. In fact I've just finished breakfast.

-I always get jumbled on the time difference.

-Not difficult, just take off five. Even a Geographer can manage that.

-And how are you keeping, my boy?

-Good. And you?

-What? Me? Oh, not too bad, well enough, you know, a bit slow on my pins, that's all. Brain still there, more or less, as far as I know. What? Missed that.

-I said we're thinking of coming over.

-To England?

-Yes, I'd like you to meet Linda.

-You're thinking of coming over? But that's marvellous.

-I want you to meet Linda.

-Linda?

-She's called Linda Shelton.

-Linda? I'd like to meet Linda.

-We're going to be married.

-Are you! Wonderful. Gosh, what news! Tell me more.

-Well, she's a musician.

-Is she! Like you. Perfect. Are you still playing the sax?

-I am. And she sings.

-And plays?

-Yes. The organ and harpsichord. And you'll never guess her favourite music.

-Go on.

-Anglican church music.

-Oh, my! You lucky boy.

-And she conducts. She conducts the choir.

-Can't wait to meet her. You must come and stay, Feeble and I would love you to, there's plenty of room, but totally understood if you'd rather not. Not stay I mean. Because I know you like your own space, you always did.

-It's not that —

-But now you're there, Paul, I just wanted to say, if I may, while we're talking, I just wanted to say, I'm sorry. Are you there? Hullo?

-Yes, I'm still here.

-Did you hear what I said?

-Look, let's talk when we meet, shall we? It's easier.

-Paul?

-Yes?

-I don't want it to be easier. The point is, a poor father, that's what I've been. I can't stop thinking of you, of the mess I made of things. It all comes back. In church, on the beach, every day it comes back.

-Does it?

-You deserved better from me. We got off on the wrong foot, somehow, didn't we, my fault entirely. You did not deserve me as a father. I regret so much, I hardly know where to begin.

-Wouldn't it be better if —

-The belittling. The denigration. The under-valuing. The ganging-up. And trying to be funny is no defence, no defence at all. Quite the opposite. There was nothing funny about it. You've gone quiet. Did you hear that?

-Yes.

-I want things to be better in the future. Between us.

-So do I.

That is the telephone call I like to think John Betjeman had in mind, and I'd like to think that he made it.

Sir John Betjeman died at his home in Daymer Lane, Trebetherick, Cornwall, on the 9th May, 1984. He is buried in St Enodoc Churchyard, near the lych gate.

Lady Penelope Betjeman, his wife, The Propellor, died in Mutisher, India, on 11th April, 1986.

Benjamin Whitrow, actor, died in London on 28th September, 2017.

Lady Elizabeth Cavendish, John Betjeman's 'other wife', Feeble, died at her home in Derbyshire on 15th September, 2018.

★

That October, a few weeks after Ben died, Bruce Young contacted me to say that Robert Bathurst had offered to take on the role of Betjeman so that we could complete the second play. I had never met Robert, let alone worked with him, but as soon as Bruce mentioned his name I could hear him playing the part. Although twenty years younger than Ben, there was something similar in their spirit and in their beguiling touch, some kinship in their nuanced amusement and English understatement.

When we did meet, Robert told me that his first professional role was in Michael Frayn's *Noises Off* in 1983, in which Ben Whitrow was the star, so they 'went back' thirty-five years. 'I started with Ben. I owe him a lot.' They even played golf together, including the course at St. Enodoc, quoting bits of Betjeman at each other as they walked from green to green along the Cornish headland. They both knew the little church.

They had both sat on 'his' churchyard bench. Both already had, I saw, inhabited the very heart of my story before I had even put pen to paper.

In November 2017, then, about two months after Ben's death, we re-gathered in the same Green Room and in the same studio, Maida Vale, MV6. It was time for us to finish the job, and, if possible, to finish it in style.

★

The plays went out on Radio 4 on Christmas Day and Boxing Day 2017. On the December 25th, at 2.15 pm, *Mr Betjeman's Class* was the programme which led up to the Queen's Speech. The whole country, in my mind's eye, Horatio, tucked into their turkey and mince pies and then settled down to listen to my play, and then, at the end, the whole country stood to attention for the National Anthem.

A day later, on Boxing Day, with the same 2.15 pm slot, it was *Mr Betjeman Regrets*, this time with two actors playing Betjeman.

56 | THE ACTORS' CHURCH

Just after lunch, on 16th February 2018, St Paul's Church, Covent Garden – commonly known as The Actors' Church – was chocker. Every seat in the seventeenth century building was taken. Everyone, it seemed, wanted to be there.

Five months after his death we had all gathered together in Bedford Street, London, to remember and to laugh again with and to pay tribute to Benjamin Whitrow. It was, you might say, a full house. Even upstairs, the west gallery was crammed.

Don't look now but isn't that Tom Courtenay, three along, on our left?

Yes.

Right behind us, don't look round, Alan Bennett.

You're the one who's looking round.

That's Catherine, Ben's wife.

End of the row in front, Prunella Scales and Timothy West.

I know, I saw them on the way in.

I love those canal programmes, don't you?

Joanna David.

Alan Price (he's going to sing). He was in The Animals. Looking in good nick, isn't he?

That's Tom, Ben's older son.

Richard Eyre. He ran the National Theatre.

Tell me something I don't know.

Patricia Hodge.

Samantha Bond.

Celia Imrie.

Ah, there's Robert Bathurst (he's going to read Betjeman's poem, Seaside Golf)

And that's, oh you know, she was in, she's in everything, yes you do know, it'll come to me in a minute.

Where's Bruce Young? He's bound to be here.

Yes, that's him, far side. Across the aisle.

Betjeman loved this Inigo Jones building, with its massive portico and columns, as in a more intimate, life-long, way he loved little St Enodoc in Trebetherick. Whether he was in North Cornwall or in the West End of London, or indeed anywhere in the world, he always found a church to visit (with a woman at his side), a church to pray in or a church to save.

And this feels a good place, the actors' church, in which to close this book on John Betjeman and Benjamin Whitrow, both actors to their fingertips.